WHAT FATE PORTENDS

A NOVEL OF THE FROST ARCANA

CLARA COULSON

KNITE
& DAY

BOOKS BY CLARA COULSON

CITY OF CROWS

Soul Breaker
Shade Chaser
Wraith Hunter
Doom Sayer
Day Killer
Spell Caster
Dawn Slayer

THE FROST ARCANA

What Fate Portends
What Man Defies
What Gods Incite
What Dawn Demands
What Dusk Divides
What Night Conceals

*To winter, whose dreariness inspired
all the snark in this book.*

CHAPTER ONE

BREAKING INTO HOUSES WAS THE HARDEST PART OF MY JOB.

You'd think the werewolves would be the hardest part, but no. The brief chases back to Kinsale with sharp teeth nipping at my heels were never particularly pulse pounding. Because I knew if they got a little too close, I could wallop the lead wolf in the face with a well-timed punch and send him crashing back into his buddies, and they'd all end up in a pile of tangled, furry limbs, snarling and whining in embarrassment. The wolf packs out in the stretches had long gone feral, and being feral made them animal-like, and being animal-like made them predictable. I evaded their blood-stained maws the way I wiped my shoes on my front-porch doormat. With ease.

The breaking and entering part was *far* more difficult.

Because it was so goddamn depressing.

I jimmied a window open like usual and climbed into a first-floor bedroom that hadn't been used in seven years.

Everything was coated in an inch of dust, and without air circulation, the recent cold rains had left the room muggy. The leak in the corner of the ceiling, water stains running down the wall, didn't help the atmosphere either, and I clicked my tongue in annoyance as I slid the window closed so nothing else would think to slip in while I was here. Just once, I'd have loved to be sent to a house that still looked warm and inviting.

Fat chance of that though.

Since most of the houses outside the protected cities were, you know, abandoned.

It was darker than usual in the house, thanks to the dense rainclouds still hanging in the sky, so I pulled a flashlight from my mostly empty satchel and clicked it on. Waving it back and forth, I searched for a scrapbook that matched the description I'd been given by my latest client. Pink. With flower designs on the plastic cover. Roughly eight inches in length and six inches in width. Contained over a hundred pictures of the Johnson family, the members of which were largely deceased.

When I didn't see the book lying around in plain sight, I checked the room in a clockwise order. First the bed. Nothing under it but shoes. Nothing beneath the mattress except a couple spiders. Then the desk. Bunch of wrinkled papers in the drawers, old bills and what not. Then the closet. Several soggy cardboard boxes stuffed with clothes, lots of mildewed dresses and suits hung up in stained bags, and a few plastic bins filled with an assortment of unique items. Trophies. Plaques. Books. Those appeared promising, so I emptied the bins out. Only to come up with zilch. There were three different cameras in the bins, but no scrapbook.

Damn. The scrapbook wasn't in this room.

Walter Johnson had said he couldn't remember where the

scrapbook had last been, only that he'd seen it two days before the nuke went off in Raleigh and he'd fled with his wife and kids, and what little supplies they could gather in the short time they had to evacuate. Irony, of course, was that the fallout never reached this far, thanks to a little magical intervention from Our Lady of Eternal Winter.

Johnson had run for nothing. And that decision had cost him nearly everything. His wife and two of his three kids had died in one of the refugee camps in Georgia during the flu epidemic. They'd have been fine if they'd just stayed put and moved to Kinsale when it gained protected status. But of course, hindsight was twenty-twenty. Most everybody had panicked in the same ignorant ways when the bombs started falling. Most everybody was still panicking now.

I left the bedroom and followed a short hall to the living room.

And here was the part of this job that always sucked the most balls.

As I shined my light across the couch and loveseat, the TV and entertainment center and coffee table, my poor, shriveled raisin of a heart started to ache at the sight of a life forgotten. On the couch was a bag of potato chips. On the coffee table, a half-eaten bowl of popcorn. On the carpet in front of the coffee table were two controllers for the video game console sitting on the entertainment center; one of them was broken where someone had stepped on it as they ran toward or away from the bedroom I'd just left.

Beyond the living room, it was even worse. There were plates and silverware set on the table in the dining room, plus a pitcher of what looked like tea adjacent to a row of dinner glasses. In the kitchen lay an island strewn with food prep items. Pots and pans. Mixing bowls. Large spoons and knives. A cutting board. Most of the actual food had rotted to nothing in the past few years, and all that remained of the final dinner the Johnsons never ate were a few stains here and there.

I hated this shit.

I hated looking at children's shoes discarded near back doors from when they'd come inside after playing in lush yards that were now frozen and dead. I hated seeing full hampers, full dishwashers, full sinks, the stark reminders of chores no one would ever return to finish. I hated seeing piles of unopened mail on countertops and side tables, the companies that mailed them no longer in existence. I hated finding half-packed bags, clothes strewn over floorboards, where people had been forced to haphazardly choose what precious things to take as they abandoned their homes for good.

I hated being forced to confront what had been, what no longer was, and what would never be again. Normal life—

I paused with one foot in the kitchen and frowned.

"Jeez, Vince," I muttered to myself. "Lighten up, will you?"

With a shake of my head, I beat back the dark, broody cloud hanging over me and resumed exploring the ground floor until I located the stairs. It took me two more tries—two young children's bedrooms whose faded wallpaper and stuffed animals made me cringe—but I finally located the master bedroom, where, as I suspected, someone had safely stowed the scrapbook away. It was sitting on the top shelf of a short bookcase. Johnson's wife had likely placed it there after adding a new picture or finding it discarded downstairs.

Crouching, I plucked it from the shelf, then tipped it open to a random page and pointed my light at it. Some of the pictures had suffered damage, while others had been sealed well enough to maintain the bulk of their features. There were even a few that looked pristine.

I tried very hard not to register the actual contents of the photos as I quickly flipped through the whole book to make sure most of them were intact enough to satisfy Johnson. They were. So I flipped the book shut, tucked it into my satchel, and made to head back downstairs at the exact pace warranted by—

A floorboard creaked.

Not exactly a rare occurrence in rundown houses. But there was something heavy to this creak, as if it was the result of added weight and not the subtle shifting of warping boards. Over the past few years of working this gig, I'd gotten pretty good at picking out the houses that only *seemed* abandoned, because squatters tended to leave little clues, like footprints in dust and objects moved in ways that made rooms feel inhabited. However, I hadn't seen any of those clues on the ground floor of this house. Which made me think either someone had followed me inside, or something had been waiting in a place I hadn't explored.

I flicked off my flashlight and stowed it away, then quietly crept over to the bedroom door. I'd left the door open a crack, so I was able to peek into the hall without making a sound. My eyes took a few seconds to adjust to the lack of light, but even when they did, I didn't find anything lurking outside the room. So I shoved my hand under the collar of my shirt and grabbed one of the star-shaped charms on my necklace, mentally whispering the words to dispel the magic I'd stuffed inside. It escaped from the charm with a subtle blue puff, like mist, and immediately, one of my glamours disappeared.

My senses sharpened fourfold.

Closing my eyes, I focused my hearing, concentrating on noises downstairs, since the top level was totally silent beyond my own pulse. At first, I didn't hear anything on the ground floor either, not even the skittering of bugs. But then, as if something had been waiting for me to pay attention, I heard a faint scraping noise. Like a nail gliding lightly across a chalkboard. Slowly. Methodically. An obvious rhythm. Too precise to be the house settling.

A chill slithered down my spine. I wasn't alone in here.

One quick glance over my shoulder told me I wouldn't be escaping out the bedroom window. Because there was a sheet of plywood nailed over it. Busting it open would make an awful racket, and the ground below was a good distance away. My gaze dropped to the floor instead, where there was an obvious water stain that I'd bet ten gem chits corresponded to the leak in the ceiling downstairs.

Stepping away from the door, I tested the integrity of the waterlogged floor. It sank under my weight pretty easily.

If I applied the right amount of force, I might be able to break straight through to the other bedroom, lower myself down, and make a mad dash for the window I'd used to enter. Close to the ground. No risk of a twisted ankle.

But that tactic would be even louder than ripping off the plywood and would immediately garner attention. Whether I'd make it out in time depended on what was lurking below.

If it was a vampire, I was fucked. They were faster than me even when I stripped my second glamour.

I checked the squishy floor one more time. *Nah. Too clunky.*

The direct approach it was then.

Back at the door, I peered out into the hall again, only to find it as empty as before. The scraping sound was still going strong, however. I tucked a finger around the edge of the door and coaxed it open, praying no rusty hinges betrayed me. When the door was nearly open wide enough to let me through, there *was* the slightest squeak, but it happened to occur at the same time as a scrape, so I didn't think it gave me away. The scraping continued undeterred. And I continued out into the hall, severely deterred, but I couldn't stand here being a wimp all day long.

So down the stairs I tiptoed, internally screaming all the way.

At the base of the stairs, which thankfully hadn't creaked too much either, it became apparent the scraping noise was coming from the kitchen. The kitchen that had been totally empty about twelve minutes prior, when I was searching the ground floor.

Oh, I didn't like that at all. Either this thing had been in the house all along, probably watching me from the shadows, or it could enter buildings with the grace of a cat. Both possibilities indicated very bad things were about to happen.

Flush against the wall of the hallway, I inched toward the edge of the kitchen entryway. I could've made a run for the back door, which was in the utility room at the end of the hall behind me. But if I turned my back on whatever was in the kitchen, and it *heard* me trying to get out, the extra second it took me to whip around could cost me my head. Literally. So it was best to take a gander at the thing I was keeping company with, see what it was so I could gauge its abilities, and *then* run away with my tail between my legs in the way least likely to get me killed.

I reached the kitchen doorway. The scraping was loud enough now that my muscles tightened in time with each repetition, a deep sense of unease skittering up and down my spine. Heart sputtering under my ribs, I had to take a deep breath to compose myself, to still the subtle quaking in my fingers, calm the pounding in my temples. I stared at the still and empty living room across from me for five long seconds. Then I poked my head past the edge of the wall.

Nosferatu was in the kitchen.

It was seven feet tall, with ash-gray skin, a bald head, a severely angular face, a hooked nose, bulbous yellow eyes, and long, pointed ears. Sticking out from its ragged, soiled, robe-like clothing were two hands that each had fingers nearly eight inches long, and one of those fingers was running its chipped black nail through a moldy stain on the surface of the kitchen island, which I assumed was all that remained of some veggie Ms. Johnson had been chopping up for dinner that fateful night.

"It" was a freaking ghoul. And it looked exactly like it had stepped out of a terrifying horror classic. Down to the crowded rows of sharp teeth nearly two inches long, that I knew from experience could bite through bone like butter. Last time I'd seen a ghoul, it had ripped a guy's arm off with those teeth while it strangled him to death with those spider-leg fingers.

Boy, that had been a bad day. I really hoped today didn't end like that.

I ducked behind the wall again, my teeth biting into my tongue as I was forced to stifle a whine. Not because I was afraid of a ghoul—if I stripped off a couple more of my glamours, I could drum up enough power to take a ghoul in a fight, no problem—but because I was afraid of *ghouls*, plural.

You see, ghouls had this funny tendency to travel in packs, so if you ever stumbled upon one ghoul, you could be sure that several more were in the immediate vicinity. And since ghouls were extremely aggressive when they fought as a pack...

A floorboard creaked behind me.

It was the exact same sound that had originally alerted me.

This time, I knew where it came from: the floorboard in front of the door that led to a room I hadn't entered. The basement. I'd opened the door to the basement when I was searching the ground floor but had elected not to go down because Walter Johnson told me the basement was for junk storage and they didn't keep anything important in there. Mentally rewinding back to the moment of that decision, I saw myself glance briefly into the darkness at the bottom of the basement stairs before I continued down the hall to see if there were any other relevant rooms on the ground floor.

I hadn't *closed* the basement door. I'd left it wide open. And in so doing, I'd woken something from its midwinter hibernation.

Several somethings.

Slowly, I peered over my shoulder. There were *nine* ghouls standing in the hallway behind me. All of them were blinking those creepy yellow eyes, no pupils, no whites, at the hapless man before them. Three of them were chomping their pointy teeth repeatedly, and when I took a hard look at their mouths, I realized they were chewing on some kind of gristle. Leftover bits and pieces from the last people they'd eaten before they'd huddled into the basement for an extended nap.

One good thing about the dreary climate shift was that a lot of supernatural creatures didn't like cold weather, so many of them had gone dormant when the long winter started. That made the stretches between the protected cities moderately safer to traverse. As long as you didn't stumble into the den of something nasty and wake it up on the wrong side of the bed. Like my dumb ass had just done.

These things probably hadn't had a meal in months, maybe years. And there I stood, just under six feet of skin and chewy muscles, bone and squishy organs, like a fucking buffet. And sure, ghouls preferred half-rotten, maggot-filled corpse meat, but they had absolutely no qualms with creating the corpses that meat came from. And—

The scraping in the kitchen had stopped.

I whipped my head back around.

Nosferatu was standing right in front of me.

I gawked at the ghoul for two-point-five seconds. Then I punched it in the face.

Its head snapped back with an audible crack, its hooked nose imploding into mush, dark green blood gushing from its wide nostrils. It bobbled, back and forth, back and forth, on its gangly legs, for what seemed like an awkwardly long amount of time, before its monster brain finally decided to send it tumbling down. It slammed into the hardwood floor with a thump that rattled every board in the living room. Then it lay there, unmoving, sluggishly blinking its big yellow eyes, like it couldn't understand I'd just sucker-punched it so hard I'd nearly broken all my fingers. (And yes, my hand was throbbing like a bitch, but I had bigger problems.)

I looked at the other nine ghouls.

They all wore similar expressions of confusion. Yellow eyes blinking in perfect unison. Bald heads cocked at the same ten-degree angle. Peeling gray lips loose around their long teeth. Their brains must've been running at half speed due to the hibernation they'd been so rudely woken from. The "extreme aggression lobes" that compelled them to rip people limb from limb hadn't yet powered up and stuck a bull's-eye to my chest.

Excellent.

I turned toward the living room again, gave a dignified nod to Nosferatu, and ran for my life.

Three strides in, when I was halfway to the couch, one of the ghouls hissed loudly, and like an echo chamber, the rest mimicked it. I bounded over the couch, propelled myself off the edge of the coffee table, and rapidly whispered the words that unraveled two more of my glamours. I landed four feet from the doorway to the bedroom I'd used as an entry point, the magic juices now flowing through my veins, wrapping around my muscles, reinforcing my bones. And just as the air parted behind me, the hairs on my neck rising, the nail of a long finger brushing the collar of my coat, the ghouls catching up in the space between breaths, super fast, super agile—I took off at ten times the speed I'd been moving before.

I crossed the bedroom in under a second, braced myself, arms up to shield my face, and propelled my body straight through the window, frame and all. Glass exploded outward, singing through the air. I soared over the entire front lawn, over the white picket fence whose paint had dulled to gray. My body, sense of balance heightened, corrected its position in midair. I landed in a rough but controlled roll and pushed myself to my feet in one smooth motion.

Nice, I thought.

Then my swinging satchel whacked me in the head.

"Goddammit," I mumbled, rubbing the aching spot above my ear as I situated my satchel back at my side and...

Hisses cut through the quiet of the gloomy afternoon.

I spun to face the front of the house.

Ghouls were spilling out of the window. Their faces were contorted into the rage of a feeding frenzy, literally frothing at the mouth.

Yep. Time to go.

I sprinted full speed down the street of what had once been a cozy suburb of Kinsale, now row upon row of abandoned, sagging houses, dead lawns, and cracking sidewalks. I'd ventured to this particular suburb a number of times since I'd become a finder of lost things, and I knew its layout well enough to navigate it blindfolded. So while the ghouls were extremely fast, they failed to close enough ground to catch me as I climbed backyard fences, leaped across empty swimming pools, bounded over a couple of sheds, and jumped the gap between the second shed and the front porch of another house. I managed to cut across the entire neighborhood in under ten minutes, my woken magic now pulsing through me, strengthening me, a growing high I had to be careful not to court too long.

The northern half of the suburb terminated at a two-lane road that cut through a dense patch of woods to join the highway that led back to Kinsale. I usually avoided this road and took the eastern route home instead because it was surrounded by flatland and I could see in every direction—see anything that might be coming after me. But today, with the ghouls still in hot pursuit, hissing and spitting and occasionally shrieking to remind me they were not giving up until I was a bloated corpse, I chose to take a gamble.

I headed north. Toward the woods. Toward the shadows that hid what lived within.

Glancing over my shoulder, I calculated the rough distance between myself and the lead ghoul—which happened to be Nosferatu, interestingly enough, with its face still leaking green blood. About eighteen feet to work with. That meant I'd have to time this budding ploy of mine with only a second or two of leeway, given that all of us were moving at the posted speed limit. I'd be cutting it close. And if my ticket out of this mess ended up coming from more than one direction?

Let's not answer that.

I pushed my legs harder, driving them against the worn asphalt under my boots, my magic urging me to call upon its entirety, to release my last three glamours so I could show those damn ghouls what a man like me could really do. I resisted the call, as I always did. Though it was difficult with my heart beating at the speed of light, sweat pouring down my face, the damp, cold air teasing me with winter's touches, like it recognized a kindred spirit in my soul. I narrowed my focus to the road before me, the trees on either side growing closer and closer, the darkness between those trees even more menacing than usual. I ran over my hackneyed plan three more times, mouthing to myself exactly what I had to do to pull this off.

You got this, Whelan. You're not that washed up. Not yet anyway.

Ten steps from the tree line, I yanked a flare gun out of my satchel, pointed it at the woods abutting the right lane, and pulled the trigger. A bright red flare burst out, shot through the air at a shallow angle, and passed perfectly between the trees for at least fifty feet before it slammed into a trunk close to the roadside and exploded in a blinding flash. The flash winked out after a handful of seconds, leaving only a rain of red sparks flickering among the shadows.

Twenty steps later, I passed the scorched tree.

Seven steps after that, the ghouls reached the tree.

At the exact same moment a werewolf leaped from the darkness.

The wolf rammed into Nosferatu with a vicious growl and snapped its powerful jaws shut around the ghoul's head. The skull exploded with a sickening squelch, green blood and grayish brain matter spraying across the asphalt. The other ghouls, infuriated at the sight of their fallen comrade, lunged at the wolf as it landed on the road, not paying attention to anything else around them. Which was why they didn't see the other wolves coming until it was too late.

An entire pack of werewolves raced out of the woods behind their leader and tore into the ghouls with abandon. Wolf teeth met ghoul flesh and flayed it from bone. Ghoul teeth met wolf flesh and ripped it to shreds. Bones cracked. Organs burst. Wolves cried. Ghouls shrieked. Gray limbs went flying. Patches of bloody fur fluttered up into the air. With so many bodies writhing in a mass of blood and gore, it was impossible to tell who was winning.

Good thing I didn't care who won.

I fled from the skirmish so fast I would've been no more than a blur flitting beneath the shadows of the trees to any human who might have seen me pass. Not that I thought there were humans out here *to* see me pass. I didn't spy a single one during my return trip. Not on the four-lane highway (unless you counted the skeletons in derelict cars). Not in any of the neglected gas stations and convenience stores and other small businesses I passed as I trekked down that highway. Not in the other two suburbs that branched off that highway, half a mile out from Kinsale proper. Nope. Not a single human soul had dared to brave the stretches today.

I didn't blame them.

Not one bit.

CHAPTER TWO

The headless horseman glared at me from atop his tall white steed. His head was sitting in his lap, beady eyes narrowed in suspicion, as his partner, an equally headless woman, waved her literal wand over my body to check for contraband magical items on my person. When her wand didn't beep—or set me on fire, or whatever it did when it declared you guilty—the female dullahan shrugged, tucked her wand into its designated band on her belt, and climbed back onto her pretty black stallion. She'd left her head perched on the saddle, and when she swung around behind it, the head started talking.

"Looks like you're clean, Mr. Whelan," she said.

Her partner's head snorted, and he added gruffly, "Surprised the wolves didn't get you today, bréagadóir, so close to the full moon. They're usually ravenous by this point in the month."

I rocked back on my heels. "No, they caught some other unfortunate fellows in my place."

He clearly assumed I meant humans, because he flashed me a haughty smirk. "Fools. Still think they're at the top of this world's food chain, don't they?"

"I find it rather pitiful myself," said the woman. "Considering how few of them were truly to blame for all this." Her arms gestured to the slate-gray sky, the rolling clouds promising another chilly rainstorm sometime later this afternoon. The sky was always gray these days, but it was typically a pale gray that allowed limited light to pass through. Just enough light to make you believe the sun was still out there somewhere, playing hide and seek.

The male dullahan rolled his eyes. "Not being an active participant in a war doesn't mean you aren't complicit in some way." He hawked a glob of spit at the ground, and it splattered on the degraded asphalt that probably wouldn't be repaired for decades. Not from a lack of roadwork crews. But from a lack of traffic.

There were no more operational gas stations because there was no longer a trade in petroleum products, so even though free cars were plentiful, due to the whole "half the human population got wiped out" thing, you couldn't drive them. They just sat there, slowly decaying. Like most things in the world.

God, what I wouldn't give to be able to make these long-ass trips in a nice, sturdy pickup.

I adjusted my satchel on my shoulder and cleared my throat. "While this is a riveting discussion, I have somewhere to be, so if you two are done hassling me, can I go in now?" I nodded toward the faintly glowing line of large symbols about ten feet behind the dullahan pair. It stretched for a mile in both directions, then curved around the east and west limits of the city, before the two ends of the line met, forming a complete circle. The protective boundary that kept the nasties in the stretches from overrunning Kinsale and killing everyone inside.

The male dullahan shrugged his broad shoulders. "Sure. Go on in. Just don't cause any trouble."

"You say that every time I come back from a trip." I kicked a loose rock his way. "You know I live here, right? I lived here even before the collapse."

His detached head sniffed in a snobbish manner. "Doesn't mean you're not a troublemaker. You're a bréagadóir after all."

"Ah, the sweet smell of prejudice in the afternoon," I drawled, marching past him. "Someone's going on my naughty list for Christmas this year. No gift for you."

Neither of them responded to that quip until I stepped over the boundary line, the tingle of insanely powerful magic washing over me like a dense blanket until I crossed the last of the symbols.

Then the female dullahan muttered to her partner, "What's Christmas again?"

"Some human holiday," the male horseman responded. "I think it's religious. Something about a guy nailed to a cross?"

Scoffing under my breath, I left the duo behind and picked up my pace as I moved into Kinsale proper. Modest office buildings, both glass walled and brick, rose up around me, interspersed with closely packed neighborhoods of townhouses, duplexes, and the occasional apartment building. Despite the gloom, only the important structures—mostly government offices, libraries, hospitals, and grocery stores—had their lights on.

There was still a major electricity shortage in Kinsale, which wasn't projected to be rectified for another eight to twelve months. Much of the power grid had been destroyed during the war, and it was a hassle to repair it when a lot of its vital parts were *outside* the city. In the stretches. Where the wild things lived.

Even so, we were making do. We still had plenty of batteries to go around, and you could use magic openly now, so lots of new products, like spell-powered lights and water heaters, were becoming common fare in the home supply shops throughout the city. After all, where there was a market for "alternative kitchen appliances," there was a wizard capitalist ready to start mass-producing magic toasters. It had only been a matter of time before the entrepreneurs began popping up.

I passed by two such entrepreneurs as I drew closer to downtown, a mom-and-pop pair who I knew as a witch and a wizard. They were busy using a levitation spell to hang up a large GRAND OPENING banner from the roof of their new store, which was brightly lit with warm yellow light cast from magic orbs attached to the walls. The hand-painted signs in the display windows promised washers and dryers that would run on single spells for a year at a time, guaranteed or your money back. They *did* look to have some nice wares inside, so I made a note of the address. My house was a little lacking in the laundry department.

A brisk wind picked up as I reached the edge of the city's main market, a tight cluster of wooden stalls and white plastic tents that stretched across four blocks of what had once been a park. The market had shut down earlier today, around lunch, after the first wave of rain and high winds swept through and drenched everyone. A few stalls had reopened, however, mostly food vendors nice enough to keep serving their usual customers, who relied on them for cheap meals.

I stopped at a stall worked by a friend of mine, Christie Bridgewater. She owned a teashop on Tillman Street but spent three days a week at the market filling canteens and water bottles with her best brews to keep people warm as they traversed the market. It was a massive loss to her bottom line, because she charged a single chit no matter the size of the container, but she did it out of the goodness of her heart.

Christie noticed me waiting as she finished up with a raggedly dressed customer, and she waved. "Hey, Vince. How's it going?" She cheerily wished farewell to the likely homeless man as he trudged off, his quaking fingers rapped tightly around his coffee mug filled with steaming tea. When he was out of earshot and no one else was in range of the stall, Christie dropped her smile and placed her hands on her hips. "What's with the cuts? Did you get into another fight while you were outside?"

"Cuts?"

She ducked down under the stall table and popped back up a second later with her purse. From it, she produced a small mirror, which she handed over to me. I held it up and viewed my face and neck. There were an assortment of thin, angry cuts on the left side.

"Oh, those," I said. "Probably happened when I jumped through the window. No worries though. Didn't even feel them."

The ability to block out mild to moderate pain was a bonus of stripping my glamours. But the cuts reminded me I needed to reassemble the three glamours I'd dropped. My senses were still heightened to nonhuman levels, and my magic, though no longer frenzied, was still buzzing through my nerves, beckoning for me to call on it again. It took me about thirty minutes to rebuild each of my glamours though, and my full concentration—complex spellwork was *hard*—so it'd have to wait until I got home.

No big deal. I could still pretend to be human with my three base glamours intact. Those were the important ones.

Christie frowned. "You jumped through a window?" She dropped her palms to the tabletop and leaned toward me. "And why, pray tell, would you choose to do that?"

I faked a cough. "Well, there was the small matter of…the horde of ghouls chasing me through a house."

"Vincent!" She whipped a stack of napkins off the table and swatted my head with them. "You shouldn't be so reckless. One day, you're going to venture into the stretches and not come back. And where will I be then?"

"Missing your Friday night Scrabble partner?"

"Precisely. We can't win the tournament against Faraday and Peterson if you're dead."

"Your concern for my well-being is touching, Chris."

She huffed, then reached for a small stack of paper cups she kept on hand in case someone didn't bring one of their own. As she filled it with black tea from her insulated beverage dispenser, she said, "But really, Vince, you need to be careful when you go out there. I know some jerks mock the job you do, but it's important to a lot of people in this town. They rely on you to retrieve the things they lost. It gives them hope, increases their morale. So you need to keep your head on your shoulders. Literally." She offered me the cup of tea. "Also, I kind of like you as a person, so I'd be a little bummed if I had to go to your funeral."

I accepted the tea with a thin smile. "Likewise. Don't get yourself killed by the tea bandit."

"Last thief who came this way, I beat with the bat I keep under this table."

"Oh yeah. I heard about that." I took a sip of the tea. I didn't get cold, even with my glamours on, as a consequence of my heritage, but I still enjoyed a good cup of hot tea. "Didn't you break his jaw?"

"And knocked out four of his teeth." She poured a second cup for herself.

"Remind me not to piss you off."

She downed the tea like a shot and slammed the cup against the table, crushing it under her palm. "How about you just don't forget it?"

I laughed. "I'll write it down."

She grinned. "It's really good to see you back in one piece. I mean it." She gestured to my satchel. "Get the goods today?"

"Yup. Exactly as ordered." I patted the bag as I finished off my tea. "I'm due for delivery in about ten minutes, so I best get going. We're meeting over at the guy's stall."

"Oh? What's he sell?"

"Watches and clocks. Used to be a jeweler, apparently." I tossed my cup over the table and heard it land in the small trashcan she always kept in the corner of her stall. "Obviously, we don't need much in the way of diamond earrings these days, so he's switched over to timepieces. He's got a lot of the traditional windup kind, from what I saw when we were chatting yesterday. Which is handy in a place where the electricity isn't reliable."

"Huh." She wiped off the table with a rag she kept tucked in her apron pocket. "I might get me one of those."

"My thoughts exactly. Half his payment for my service is a nice mantel clock. It looks like an authentic antique. Might be worth something thirty years from now, when the world has an actual economy again."

"Ha! Now there's a nice dream." She made a shooing motion. "Off you go. Get paid. Earn your keep. You can show me the clock next time we have Scrabble night at your house."

"It's a date." I gave her an exaggerated wink.

"You wish, Whelan. Keep walking."

I ambled off with a smirk on my face, navigating through the complex maze of stalls until I found the white tent that housed Walter Johnson's humble business. He was sitting at a small table in the tent, tinkering with a pocket watch. He glanced up at the sound of me moving the tent flap out of my way, and started at the sight of the courier he'd sent out into the stretches. I got the impression from the way the color drained from his face that he hadn't really believed I'd come back.

Not everyone knows you aren't fully human, I reminded myself.

"Did you find it?" He sat his tools and the watch on the table and rose from his rickety stool. "Was it intact?"

I opened my satchel, slid out the scrapbook, and offered it to him. "Item as described. One scrapbook containing family pictures in fair condition."

He snatched the book from me and flipped through it, stopping only when he came to a page plastered with photos from a child's birthday party. He ran his fingers tenderly over the plastic cover protecting a picture of his entire family holding up slices of cake. Judging from the date marked on the page in sparkly stickers, the photo had been taken the summer before the purge started. A few months before everything went to shit. The party was probably one of the last fun family get-togethers the Johnsons ever had.

Walter Johnson blinked back tears as he closed the book. "It's perfect. Thank you." He clutched the scrapbook to his chest as he crouched to retrieve a box and a chit bag from under his worktable. As he stood back up, knees cracking under his weight, he offered both items to me. "I packaged your clock for you. And the bag contains the agreed-upon five hundred chits."

I tucked the box under my arm, then shook the bag to hide a subtle pinch of magic that let me count the exact amount of gem chits inside it. Five hundred exactly. And they were in big denominations, twenties and fifties, which made me think Johnson had taken out a loan. Because most small shop owners dealt exclusively in fives and tens, due to their less-than-rich clientele.

I would've felt bad about leaving the guy's wallet full of dust, but I had to make a living too, and I could only do three or four runs a month before my luck ran out and I ended up in a situation like the ghoul mess. I *had* to charge a risk premium.

If I took too many trips outside, I really would end up dead.

"Say," Johnson muttered as he hugged the scrapbook tighter against his chest, "what did the house look like? Was it still in good condition?"

I figured it would be a bad idea to mention a group of flesh-eating monsters had taken up residence in the basement of the house he'd lived in before most of his family died, so I replied, "A little water damage from the continual storms. But otherwise, I think it's pretty much like you left it." I also elected not to mention the window I destroyed. "Anything else you need?"

"No, no." He gave me his best attempt at a smile. "You can go, Mr. Whelan. Again, thank you so much for retrieving the scrapbook. It means a lot to me and Rebecca." Rebecca was his only surviving child. She was fourteen, and he'd brought her along to our initial meeting in an obvious attempt to guilt me into lowering my prices. Didn't work. "She'll be so happy to see this," he continued. "She took some of these pictures herself."

"Glad to hear that. All in a day's work." I backtracked to the tent flap and patted the top of the box as I slipped through. "Thanks for the clock. I'll put it to good use. See you around, Mr. Johnson."

When the tent flap closed behind me, he was still hugging the scrapbook for dear life.

Poor bastard. Him and all the others like him.

CHAPTER THREE

Flannigan's was lit with lantern light. It gave the place an "ancient pub" ambiance I enjoyed, and the deep shadows between the oil lanterns on each table made anonymity a breeze. So I strolled in, buffeted by another cold gale, and wound through the crowded tables toward the bar, where O'Shea was drying a few mugs and replacing them on the shelf near the taps. I took my usual seat at the very end of the bar, sat my clock box on the stool next to me, and tapped four times on the bar top. O'Shea perked up at the sound, then quickly finished with his current mug before he spun around to face me.

"Well, look what the wind blew in," he said in his deep rumble of a voice. "Was starting to think the stretches got the better of you today, my friend. You're half an hour later than usual."

I gestured to the tap behind him, which contained my favorite beer, produced right here in Kinsale. The brewery was one of the few businesses that hadn't shut down during the war. Even when nukes were raining from the sky, and faeries were toppling world governments, people were still chugging beer by the keg. "Left a little later than usual," I said as the bartender grabbed the same mug he'd just dried and filled it to the top. "I actually made really good time getting back. Though that was more a matter of necessity."

O'Shea slid my beer over to me and slung his white drying rag over his shoulder. His gaze focused on the left side of my face, where the cuts were, and he smiled. "Got yourself into a jam, did you?"

"Also got myself out of one"—I took a sip of the delicious brew—"which I think is the more impressive feat."

He snorted. "What was it this time? More werewolves?"

"Ghouls."

"Ugh." He screwed his face into a sneer. "Nasty fuckers. They ate a cousin of mine a few years back, you know?"

"Really?"

"Yep." He proceeded to tell me a story about his cousin "Paul," who got killed during one of the big riots in Raleigh some months before the nuke leveled it. About eighty people died when the National Guard fired indiscriminately into the crowd, and in the aftermath, their bodies were collected by the authorities, likely to identify them in order to place their entire families on the "terrorist watch list." Except the government never got the chance to exercise its authoritarian thumb. Because the warehouse where they'd stored the bodies got overrun by ghouls, who proceeded to eat most of the corpses. "Yeah," O'Shea finished, "when his parents finally got his remains, it was only an arm, a leg, and his head. They had a closed-casket funeral."

"Did the parents survive the war?" I asked after taking a long chug from my mug.

"Nope," he replied. "Every member of my family except my sister and Uncle Manny died when the bombs fell."

"Sorry to hear that, pal."

He shrugged. "I got the same sob stories as everybody else. No point in dwelling on them. We can't all stew in depression. There are too many jobs to do. Somebody's got to keep the world spinning until the winter ends."

"I like your attitude. We need more of that." I raised my mug in deference to him. "And I love the fact you think beer is vital to the restoration of human civilization."

"Is it not?" He smirked at me, then turned to serve another patron who'd shuffled up to the bar to order a pitcher for his table.

When the patron ambled off with the goods in tow, I said, "Any news come through on the wire?" O'Shea had eyes and ears all over town, courtesy of being the guy everybody spilled their guts to when they were having a bad day. So whenever strange things started happening in the shady corners of the city, O'Shea was one of the first people to find out about it.

He wiped off the bar top with his rag before he leaned close to me and spoke softly. "Been a few more disappearances than normal. People up and vanishing in the middle of the day. No witnesses. No suicide notes. No one spotted going beyond the barrier by any of the boundary guards. Haven't noticed a pattern to it yet. Young. Old. Male. Female. A mixed bag. Only thing they have in common is they're human."

Finishing off my beer with a long draw, I sat my empty mug on the bar top and replied, "I'll look into it when I have a chance. Maybe something's slipped through the barrier, started picking people off the streets. If you get me a list of the missing, I'll do a little digging, see if I can find some clues to drop in front of the cops. Get them sniffing so they'll actually do their jobs."

"This city would be better off if you were still a cop, Vince."

I opened my mouth to retort, but O'Shea produced that hard, steady look he smacked you with when you were about to do something stupid. So I swallowed the bitter words and said instead, "I don't disagree with you, buddy, but the status quo of that situation isn't going to change, no matter how much wishful thinking you use to try and scrub the blood off the concrete."

O'Shea dipped his head. "I know. It's just a damn shame is all. We need someone like you helming the force, not those cowards with badges who quake in their boots at the first sign of a paranormal criminal. They don't have what it takes to police this brave new world."

"You'll have to take your complaints up to management. Because I'm too low on the totem pole to effect that sort of change." I slipped off the barstool and glanced at the tinted windows at the front of the room. The sky was spitting rain now, and the wind had picked up even more, bending the skinny trees planted along the sidewalks and whipping up paper trash from the gutters.

"Too low on the totem pole?" O'Shea quirked an eyebrow. "You sure about that?"

I halted with one hand halfway to my coat pocket, in which I'd stowed the bag of gem chits Walter Johnson gave me. Beer sat heavy in my unsettled gut as I met O'Shea's eye. Lots of folks in this town knew I wasn't fully human—many people had some nonhuman ancestry, as society had discovered during the purge, so it wasn't a huge shocker—but almost none of them knew *exactly* what I was, and O'Shea wasn't counted among the tiny number who did. Yet I could tell from the way he regarded me, a subtle accusation in the thin line of his lips, nothing malicious about it, just percep-tive, that something I had said or done over the past few years of our frequent bar encounters had given me away.

I shifted on my feet, discomfort roiling in my chest like reflux. "Look—"

O'Shea held up his hand. "No apologies needed. And I won't tell anyone. Just wanted you to know that I knew, be-cause I get the sense you're the sort of guy who likes to keep track of the people who *really* know him."

The anxiety wound tight around my ribs loosened a smid-gen. I let out a haggard breath. "No apologies needed maybe, but I feel like I should give you one anyway. It's not that I like deceiving people, it's…"

"I know how it is. No big thing." He gave me a dismissive wave. "Though I do admit I'm curious about why you under-sell yourself as much as you do."

"That's complicated," I said lamely.

O'Shea smiled. "Isn't it always?"

A shrill gust rattled the open shutters on the windows.

"You should get on home," he added, snatching up my empty mug. "Looks like this storm is going to be a doozy."

I gave him my best grateful smile, which I assumed looked something like a shriveled worm on a sidewalk. "See you later, man. Stay safe."

"I always stay safe, Whelan. You're the only madcap here."

"Nah, you got it all wrong," I said as I backed toward the door. "I'm the most cautious person you'll ever meet."

With that, I slipped out into the building storm.

The shortcut home wasn't my favorite route, but with a frigid downpour blowing in, black clouds on the horizon, I wanted to hurry along, lest my new clock get ruined before I even had a chance to use it. The reason I disliked the shortcut was because it took me past my old house, the cozy one-story with a cute front porch where I'd spent many a summer reading books and taking naps and sipping beers in the evening, waving to all who walked by. It was my ancestral home, my father's place before he died of a stroke two years before the purge.

I'd inherited the house just like I'd inherited his job.

Unfortunately, I'd let both those legacies go to shit.

As I cut a corner onto North Lily, the little house came into view. The white siding. The red shutters. The decorative fence. The mass of obscene graffiti that had been painted over all those once pretty features. The scorch marks on the panel siding from that time someone threw a Molotov cocktail at the living room window. The cracked brick along the bottom from where someone had taken a hammer to it. The ribbons that remained of the porch screening. Someone had even kicked the fence and bent it in a couple places.

All that damage had occurred after I'd been outed to the public as a paranormal and forced to go underground. But I hadn't found out about it until I emerged from hiding when the US government fell to the very creatures they were persecuting and faerie rule became the law of the land. I returned home to find my father's pride and joy destroyed, inside and out. The mobs had broken in and ruined all my belongings too.

The sight of that wrecked house always made my blood

boil. Not because I cared about where I lived, but because the damage was the equivalent to spitting on my father's grave. He'd been one of the most respected members of the Kinsale community, a decorated police veteran, honored by the mayor, a hero to the people. And they'd gone and defaced his memory as much as they'd defaced his house. All because his son had a nonhuman mother.

One day, I would fix that house. When resources were plentiful again, and the weather wasn't shit. I'd make it the prettiest damn house in the whole neighborhood. And I'd ward it to the teeth, so that anyone who so much as stepped on the lawn without my permission would get blown to kingdom come.

Until that far-off day though, I'd have to let the fury smolder.

I trudged down the sidewalk with heavy steps, forcing myself to look the other way, at all the other derelict houses in the neighborhood. With the number of refugees trickling into Kinsale, most of these houses would be inhabited eventually, but...

A flash of white in the corner of my eye caught my attention. I paused and looked to the bent fence in front of my old house. Someone had taped a piece of paper to one of the fence poles. Within the last couple hours, it must've been, because the paper was still dry.

I crouched down to get a better view of the complex array of writing scrawled in blue ink across the small square. And I immediately recognized it for what it was: a magic charm. Not just any magic charm either, but a conflagration charm.

Those tended to create a ball of flame roughly the size of a horse.

With half my glamours down, I could see the tiny threads of magic sewn into the paper, sparkling like a spider's web in bright light. The charm was armed much like a grenade, and if someone triggered it—by touching the fence—they'd get consumed by a superheated blast faster than they could scream. It was extremely dangerous, reckless, and stupid to leave such a powerful charm sitting out here where anyone could bump into it by accident.

I had no idea why someone would put a charm like this on the fence, considering the house behind it was clearly abandoned, and frankly, I didn't care. I couldn't leave it here. So I called up a few tendrils of my own magic and directed them to encompass the square of paper.

My energy ghosted across the inked symbols, leaving trails like curls of frost. The charm sensed the intrusion into its construction and attempted to ignite, but it was too slow. My spell gummed up the "gears" of the charm before it could do any harm, and it ended up in a frozen state, unable to explode, unable to abort—unable to dispel the magic signature embedded within that would allow me to track it back to its source.

Charm contained, I plucked the paper off the fence, folded it up, and tucked it into my coat pocket. *Some witch or wizard in this town is going to get a stern talking-to*—another vicious gust shrieked through the neighborhood and nearly blew me over—*sometime tomorrow, when there aren't any gale-force winds in the forecast.*

I continued down the street and cut diagonally across four more blocks, a direct path to my "new" house, the house I'd lived in for the past six years. It had once been an antique store with a second-floor apartment, and it'd been owned by a sweet elderly couple who died in the collapse. I'd bought it for the bargain price of free, because the mass exodus from Kinsale in the immediate aftermath of the Raleigh nuking had left even the nicest homes in the city standing vacant. And most of their original owners had never returned.

The house wasn't large or luxurious, but it was sturdy, clean, well insulated, fully furnished, and already had a storefront built into it. Which was exactly what I needed.

I deactivated my wards, unlocked the front door, and slipped inside just as the first wave of torrential rain crashed into Kinsale. I shut the door behind me, relocked it, and reactivated my wards, which would electrocute anyone who tried to set foot in my house by force. Couldn't be too careful these days, with headless horsemen guarding the city and ghouls running wild in the stretches and assholes trying to steal doorknobs from the box of spares I had near the front of the store, thinking the metal could be traded for gem chits.

The entire store was filled with stuff. It was a stuff store. Tons of odds and ends on every shelf, in every bin, piled high everywhere I could fit anything that someone might want to buy. I had hinges to go with the doorknobs, mirrors to go on your walls, about three hundred flashlights of varying sizes, and enough batteries to work them all. I had blankets for sale, pillows and comforters too, most of them still in their original packaging. I had books and old magazines. CDs and CD players. Radios of all shapes and sizes. If it was something you'd need to replace in these trying times, I probably sold it.

And yes, I'd stolen *everything*. From Walmart and Target and Lowe's and every other big-box store in a twenty-five mile radius of Kinsale. But, you see, people didn't get to judge me for "looting" because I'd taken it all from the stretches. Which they were too scared to enter because there were thousands of things roaming around out there that liked to eat people. So they paid me reasonable sums to replace the things that they could no longer easily buy, since every big-box store had gone out of business when countries started slinging ICBMs at each other.

It wasn't exactly a lucrative business, this store, because I tended to undercharge the truly desperate—and there were a lot of truly desperate in Kinsale—but I didn't need the sales. The store was just a big advertisement for my far more profitable job, which was explained in the big poster I'd stuck in the front window:

LEAVE SOMETHING PRECIOUS IN THE STRETCHES?

I CAN GET IT BACK!

See inside for details.

A piece of tape on the sign had come unstuck again, I noticed as I wiped my shoes off on the mat. So I reached over and slapped the flapping corner back into place on the glass and made a mental note to add another strip of tape later. Then I navigated through the densely packed shelving units and boxes and bins until I reached the checkout counter, pushed through the little half-door into the "employee-only" space, and swung around to the full door that opened onto the stairs leading to the second floor. But as I was digging around in my pockets for the key that opened said door, I heard a sound.

Knocking.

I glanced over my shoulder...and raised an eyebrow.

Because a young guy in three-quarters of a suit was standing outside in the rain, getting utterly drenched in the downpour. When he caught me looking his way, he waved at me enthusiastically, despite the fact he was literally standing in front of the sign suction-cupped to the door that said CLOSED in big red letters.

For a moment, with a hand in my pocket, one finger touching the key that would let me upstairs, where I could settle in for the night with a good book and some fuzzy blankets, I strongly considered leaving the guy out in the rain.

Lucky for him, I wasn't that big an asshole.

It remained to be seen whether that was also lucky for me.

CHAPTER FOUR

THE GUY IN THE SUIT, WHO INTRODUCED HIMSELF AS "TOM," stood in front of my counter, a puddle of water growing around his feet. His tan suit vest and pants were plastered to his body, and the white shirt he had on was totally transparent, revealing even more of his chilled skin. He was covered in goose bumps and shaking like a leaf, and the edge of his lips were a somewhat disconcerting shade of blue. If I had to guess, I'd say he was about twenty-one, going by the baby face and the big hazel eyes that were giving me that pleading look I hated. Oh, and the fact he was naïve enough to run around outside in a magic-powered winter rainstorm. Only dumb kids and dumb*asses* did that.

As he tried to compose himself and stop quaking long enough to get a coherent sentence out, I shuffled over to a shelf piled high with towels, snatched one off the top, and tossed it his way. "Dry yourself off, kid. You look like a drowned rat."

He unraveled the towel and started rubbing down his face and hair. "T-Thank you, s-sir," he stammered out.

"Don't thank me yet. That towel's not free. I want it back before you go, unless you want to pay for it."

The rain battering the rooftop grew heavier, so much so it sounded more like hail.

"Though I do have ponchos for two chits," I added, "if you'd like to refrain from drowning on your way home."

Tom gave me a sheepish grin. "S-Sorry for s-showing up at such a bad time. But I have kind of an urgent request."

"Request?" I jutted my thumb toward the back of my advertising poster, which had come partially unstuck from the window yet again. "Something you want out in the stretches?"

"Um, not exactly." He ran a hand through his damp hair. "I believe the item I'm looking for is actually here, in Kinsale."

I leaned against my counter, arms crossed. "Then why don't you go get it yourself?"

"Because"—he worried his lip while he thought how to best phrase a request he knew I was going to loathe—"it was taken by black-market scavengers."

Ah. Now I get it.

There was a thriving black market in Kinsale, largely run by elements of organized crime, some of which had survived the collapse, some of which had cropped up after Kinsale became a protected city. The underground marketplaces and bootleg shops around the city sold a large variety of goods recovered from beyond the boundary, kind of like I did, but there was a significant difference between their wares and mine. The black market prospered from selling luxury goods pilfered from the empty homes of the now dead rich and famous.

Black-market organizers employed "scavenger packs,"

gangs of foolhardy gold seekers, mostly humans packing guns, who ventured out into the stretches way more frequently than me to recover all the once prized possessions of the one percent. Expensive jewelry. Priceless paintings and sculptures. Designer-label clothing, purses, and shoes. I'd heard a rumor that one pack had managed to tow an antique sports car in mint condition a full fifteen miles through the stretches—at which point they got attacked and eaten by ravenous werewolves.

Scavenger packs had exceedingly high turnover rates.

The risk was apparently worth the reward though. There were just enough wealthy people in Kinsale to keep the gem chits flowing like honey through those underground rivers.

Generally, I didn't give a hoot about the black market, and they didn't give a hoot about me. To the mobsters of Kinsale, I was just that weirdo who got his jollies off by recovering junk from middle-class homes and making people cry from the power of nostalgia. I wasn't a threat to their bottom line, so they ignored me. Literally. I'd run into scavenger packs twice during my trips over the past few years, and both times, none of those schmucks even acknowledged my existence.

Didn't really bother me though. They stayed in their lane, I stayed in mine, and we all got along just fine. I didn't go poking dragons that didn't try to roast me first.

Which was why my immediate response to the half-drowned kid was, "No."

He was taken aback. "But I d-didn't even say what the item is."

"You don't have to. Your item's not in the stretches. I advertise item recovery *from* the stretches, not from criminals running underground trade rings inside Kinsale."

Tom pouted. It made him look about twelve. "Please, Mr. Whelan—"

"Don't make me repeat myself." I nodded toward the door. "Take your pity party somewhere else. Or better yet, keep it to yourself. If you go running your mouth too loud about the activities of the local mafia, you're going to vanish off the face of the Earth, until someone finds your half-eaten corpse in the stretches a few months from now."

Tom wrung his hands in the towel and closed his eyes. For a second, I thought he was actually going to be smart and listen to me and walk out in defeat. Then, as he released a deep sigh, he slipped his hand inside his vest and pulled out from a hidden interior pocket a stack of long, thin objects wrapped in brown leather and secured with a black spandex tie. He sat the stack on my countertop, undid the knot from the tie, and unwrapped the leather to reveal…twenty thousand-chit bars.

I gawked at the thin sapphire bars, my jaw stuck so far open I could've swallowed a tennis ball. The last time I'd seen so much money in one place, I'd been a rookie detective investigating the death of a bank security guard, who'd been shot dead during a violent heist. He'd grabbed one of the money bags as the robbers were fleeing, and held on to it even though he was shot nine times. After a considerable amount of yanking between the robber and the guard, the bag tore wide open, and hundred-dollar bills went flying everywhere. The poor guard bled to death lying atop more money than he made in his entire career.

The same off-kilter feeling I had then, standing before a dead man surrounded by bloody Benjamins, overcame me now. *What the ever-loving fuck?*

I snapped at Tom, who was obviously more than he appeared, "What kind of scam is this?"

"No scam, Mr. Whelan," he replied, still sounding timid and cold. "I swear. I just really want the harp back, and I can't get it myself. I've already tried—and miserably failed."

"Harp?"

He slung the towel over his shoulder and straightened his posture, trying to project an air of confidence that didn't come naturally. "It belonged to an aunt. She lived in Adelaide, about twenty miles north of here. She was actually part of an orchestra, though she played the violin, not the harp. The harp was considered an heirloom, having come into the family about five generations prior. It was appraised about ten years ago and found to be worth a substantial sum because it was quite old and had historical value. Shortly before the war, several different museums were vying for it."

"Museums that don't exist anymore," I threw in.

"That's not the point." He scratched the back of his neck. "I don't care *who* wants to buy it or for how much. The harp is of great significance to my family legacy, and I want it back." He tapped a finger against one of the chit bars. "And as you can see, I'm willing to pay quite a large sum to reclaim it."

"That's a lot of money for a musical instrument, kid. Especially in these times."

"It's my money." He pursed his lips. "I can spend it how I want. And I want the harp."

The negative reaction I'd had to the sight of the chits began to unwind, and I blew out a breath through my teeth. "Why come to me? If you're one of those rich brats who live over in Rosewood Estates, surely you can afford the best guy in town for this job. Someone more literate with black-market operations than me."

"Wrong." He shook his head. "You're the best man for the job. *Because* you're not involved in the black market. And because you used to be a detective. You're good at solving mysteries and you're experienced with managing and subverting criminals. With your skill set, I think you can do exactly what I need you to in a timely manner."

"What do you mean?" I shifted my weight. "This have to do with you failing to get the harp back yourself?"

"That's exactly it." He sighed. "I actually located the harp, thanks to a tip from an acquaintance of mine who attends black-market auctions regularly. He saw it listed among the new arrivals to be auctioned in coming weeks. But by the time I managed to get invited to an auction myself—you have to schmooze with the right people—it was too late. Someone had already bought the harp. The problem is, I don't know *who* purchased it because the organizers keep all the auction records private."

"Wait, so you don't want me to actually *get* the harp for you?"

"The job's not but so dangerous, Mr. Whelan." He laughed nervously. "I'm not trying to get you killed. What I want is for you to acquire the information I can't: the name and address of the person who bought the harp. To do that, you'll need to temporarily gain access to the auction organizers' buyer list ledger, which is kept locked in a safe at all times. Except during the auctions. At last Wednesday's auction, I tried to bribe my way into getting a look at the ledger, but I was rebuffed. The guards were too scared of their bosses to risk retribution. They kicked me out of the building and blacklisted me from future auctions."

"I do believe I already said I don't like kicking hornets' nests." I tapped my foot on the tile floor. "If I get caught like you did, I'll have mobsters giving me the stink eye. I don't need that kind of attention."

He pulled the towel from his shoulder and started to fold it up. "Look, I know it's asking you to take on more personal risk than you usually do, but I'm willing to pay a decent premium for your services." He gestured to the gem chits again. "That's a down payment. I'll pay you the other half if you manage to track down the harp for me."

I actually took a step back. "You're willing to pay me *forty thousand* chits, not even to get this harp back but just to tell you where it is?"

"The harp is worth a great deal more than forty grand, in actual monetary terms and in sentimental ones. So, yes. If you can find the harp for me, I'll pay you every chit." He slid the pile of sapphire bars toward me, then gave me his best teary-eyed puppy expression. "Please, Mr. Whelan. The harp is all that's left of the family, besides a few rotting houses in the stretches. It would mean so much to me if you could find out who bought it."

"And what are you going to do with that information?" I asked.

"I'd like to negotiate a buyout or trade to get the harp back. Nothing crazy. Just a good old-fashioned business arrangement."

Huh. That almost sounds reasonable.

I weighed my options. It was a stupid idea to risk myself by stepping on the toes of the mob, but at the same time, forty thousand chits would go a long way. That much dough would give me a cushy rainy day fund, if something ever happened to my "new" house, or if I ever had to split and run to another protected city because I pissed off the wrong powerful being.

I usually bled people's wallets dry running this lost-and-found gig of mine, and I only charged a thousand to fifteen hundred a pop (or occasionally bartered for goods of roughly equal value). I could make almost a year's worth of income from this one job alone, thanks to Mr. Moneybags here. And I wouldn't even be tempted to feel guilty about taking so much, because he clearly had more where that came from, if he was planning to *buy* the harp back.

God, this was tempting.

Play it safe or roll the dice?

I looked from the pile of high-value gem chits to Tom's pitiful baby face, looked back to the chits, looked back to the baby face, looked back to the chits, took a brief detour through an existential crisis where I questioned the underlying principles of my morality, and then looked back to Tom. "All right," I said. "I'll find out who bought your harp."

"Yes!" Tom threw his hands into the air, and was about to jump up and down like a joyful child when he realized how silly that would be. He awkwardly cleared his throat, dropped his hands, and pretended to smooth out his sopping wet suit as he spoke. "Thank you so much. Here's my phone number." He pulled a surprisingly intact scrap of paper from his pocket and sat it next to the pile of chits. There was a number scrawled on it in black ink, still legible despite a few smudges. "Please don't hesitate to call me. Any time of day. I want to know as soon as you find the harp."

"Will do." I stepped to the side and bent down, pulling a cardboard box out from under a low shelf. The box was full of clear plastic ponchos folded into small squares. I grabbed one and offered it to him. "I think you've paid more than enough for this job to get one of these on the house."

He produced a squeak of a laugh and took the poncho, handing me the towel in exchange. "Awesome. I will definitely need this."

I turned to face the front windows. The rain had lightened somewhat, but it was still coming down in sheets. Two inches of water stood on the road, and rapids rushed through the gutters, spiraling down into the storm drains like whirlpools. "I know it was a joke, but…you don't really live in Rosewood, do you? That's a hell of a long walk from here in this weather."

"Oh, no worries." He slid the poncho out of its package and shook it open. "I have a friend who lives about eight blocks from here. I can stop by her place and wait out the storm. Sleep over if it doesn't let up. She won't mind."

"But you *do* live in Rosewood?" It was the most expensive, and secure, neighborhood in town, courtesy of being a gated community with a heavily warded fence. It catered to what was left of the wealthy elite from the world before the collapse, and the nouveau riche who had risen at the dawn of the reconstruction. Lots of big business owners, highly skilled professionals, the usual suspects. With the suit and the giant stash of chits, Tom seemed like he fit right in with that crowd.

But he refused to answer my question, admit to his economic status.

He did blush though, which was just as telling.

"Right." I gestured to the door. "If you don't need anything else, I've had a long day, and I'd really like to settle in for the evening…"

"Of course! I apologize for disturbing you. I shouldn't have barged in like I did. Very rude." He slid the poncho over his head. It fell all the way to his ankles. "Have a good night, Mr. Whelan."

Tom scuttled off across the store and plunged back into the heart of the storm. He was almost swept away by a big gust of wind, but he managed to keep his footing and trundle on down the road. I walked over to the door and watched him go until he turned a corner two blocks down and vanished into the murk. Then I locked the door yet again, reactivated my wards, and returned to the counter. Where my literal fortune awaited.

I pinched one of the chit bars between two fingers and held it up. It wasn't counterfeit. But chit bars of such high value were almost never seen in general circulation, because most people didn't make a thousand chits in a month. This kid's family must've left behind a lot of critical assets—he probably owned a working factory or something—for him to have amassed so much money under the new currency system in so few years. *And he's willing to blow a huge chunk of it on a harp.*

The things people did in the name of nostalgia never ceased to amaze me.

CHAPTER FIVE

I WOKE UP WITH A CRICK IN MY NECK. I'D FALLEN ASLEEP IN my reclining chair, and my head had tilted sharply to one side. So I spent the first ten minutes of my morning kneading the sore spot before I stood up and shambled over to my bathroom. I'd been working on rigging a complex series of charms to run the water heater and the bathroom lights. But I hadn't quite worked out all the kinks yet—I'd gotten electrocuted last time I tried to take a shower—so I flicked on my battery-powered lantern, then filled the tub with water and heated it using a simple spell instead.

I could've just weathered the cold water, of course, since I didn't feel cold temperatures, but I enjoyed a nice, hot bath as much as I did a cup of steaming tea. It was relaxing, and having hot water made the world seem a little less dreary. You know, for like fifteen minutes.

Stripping off yesterday's dirty clothes, I dropped them in

a pile in the corner and retrieved a fresh towel and washcloth from under the sink. As I was straightening up, the lantern light glinted off the helix-shaped scars running horizontally across my back and arms, reflecting with a flash in the mirror above the sink. I should've looked away, because the sight of the scars always put me in a bad mood, but today, I couldn't stop myself from tracing them with my eyes. They made a complete circle, continued all the way around my chest, bisecting my ribcage with curved white marks that stood out on my skin.

Iron scars.

Echoes of pain and blurry memories flashed across the forefront of my mind, taunting voices at their edges, urging me to hurt and die. They triggered a visceral fury that began to build inside my chest like steam about to shriek, and…

My reflection in the mirror faded as crackling frost coated the pane.

Shit. I pulled myself away from the anger and kicked it back to the dark corner of my soul where it belonged. The frost immediately dissipated, the abrupt burst of cold leached away by the rising warmth of the tub water.

I touched my chest and realized I'd left my necklace of glamour charms sitting on the side table in the living room after I finished rebuilding the three I broke yesterday. The charms were still effective at a distance, but they were easier for my wily magic to subvert when they weren't physically touching me. Particularly in instances of emotional upheaval.

I took a quick trip back to the living room and put the necklace on. Last thing I needed was some hapless human getting a glimpse of my true self if I got pissed off. They'd run and tell the whole damn city what I was, and then I'd *really* be ostracized. I may not have had too many friends these days, but the ones I did have were good company. It'd suck to lose them like I'd lost so many others. Very few people were as understanding as O'Shea.

Charms fully functional again, I finally sank into the hot water and lay back to enjoy a good soak before my busy day got started.

An hour later, I was strolling down Hayburn Street, a crowded neighborhood of duplexes with low-priced room rentals popularly used as transition housing for new arrivals. Squalor permeated the area, from the alleys overflowing with black bags to the thick layers of foul-smelling grime on the sidewalks and front stoops, to the boarded windows, many with broken panes. Feral cats roamed the street, eating food scraps from torn trash bags and lounging on any dry space they could find. One of them, an orange tabby, followed me for two blocks, until it found another passerby to bother.

Children with bright, frightened eyes left out on the stoops to amuse themselves watched me in curiosity as I turned right into a tiny courtyard between two buildings with brick façades that had started to crumble years ago. The faux-gothic fence that separated the courtyard from the sidewalk was made of wrought iron, but the gate was open, so I didn't have to touch it. (I wore gloves in case I had to handle iron, but it still stung a bit through the fabric.) I strolled on in, following the brick path around a nonfunctional stone fountain and avoiding large puddles from yesterday's storm. At the very back of the courtyard, abutting a tall brick wall, was Mo's one-stop supply shop.

Though "shop" was a generous term. It was just three tables with a blue tarp pitched over them, where Mo sold basic supplies for inflated prices to people who'd just arrived in Kinsale with nothing but the clothes on their backs. You could get the same stuff cheaper at my store, and Mo often did. He came in once a month and made a large purchase; he would then resell my wares on Hayburn with huge markups. The processing center for refugees was only a quarter mile up the street, so many of them passed this way as they went on the hunt for housing and other necessities.

I would've been appalled at such a lack of integrity once upon a time, and probably thrown the book at a crook like Mo. But I didn't feel much in the way of outrage for people getting fleeced by greedy opportunists. If someone came begging to *me*, I'd throw them a bone for old times' sake, because I was nice like that. But if someone like Mo dangled the bone over their head instead? *Eh.* I didn't have enough sympathy left in my well to really care. The purge had almost drained it dry.

Mo was at the end of one table, counting out chits and sorting them into bags in his lockbox, when I walked over. He glanced up at me—and did a double take. "Whoa! Whelan. Not the guy I was expecting."

"I assume you were expecting your drug dealer?"

Mo was a short bald guy with a thick neck, and when he blushed, his entire head turned bright red. He looked like a tomato as he answered, "You know I kicked that habit months back."

"Yes, but how many habits have you started since then?" I flicked my eyes toward a couple of malnourished people in virtual sacks picking through boxes of clothes one table down. "You planning to jumpstart their habits today?"

He rubbed a five-chit piece between his thumb and forefinger, a nervous habit. "Not them in particular."

"Uh-huh."

"Look, Whelan, what do you want?" He raised both arms to gesture to the area behind the tables, where he had most of his inventory loaded into plastic bins. "I already bought a shit ton of stuff from you this month, and I know you're not hurting for cash because a couple of my buddies saw you come in from the stretches yesterday, which means you just got paid for a big job. So why are you hassling me?" He squinted. "You didn't rejoin the cops, did you?"

"Hell no." I picked up a box of brightly colored plastic straws from a wicker basket next to the lockbox and shook it. Half empty. He'd been selling them piecemeal. What a weasel. "Actually, I was planning to pay you—for some choice information."

"Huh?" He cocked a bushy eyebrow. It was weird how he had such thick eyebrows but no hair on his head. "What kind of information?"

"I have it on good authority that you occasionally help out with staffing at certain exclusive auctions run by certain unlawful people that sell certain expensive and unique items, due to your previous occupation as a private security expert." I sat the straws back in the basket, leaned forward, and lowered my voice. "I'll pay you five hundred chits if you tell me where the next auction is taking place."

Mo balked. "No way, man. If you cause trouble at an auction, and one of the big bosses finds out it was me who—"

I raised a finger to silence him. "You think I'd give you up to any mobster in this town? You think I'd give anyone up? You think I'd give any*thing* up? Mo, I'd march backward into hell flipping two birds and cursing in French before I'd give an inch to one of those bitches, much less a mile. I might not be a cop anymore, but I'll be damned if I do anything but spit in the face of a crime lord."

Mo shrank in on himself, cowed. "I know you wouldn't give me away intentionally. I didn't mean to imply that. But you've got to know these people employ certain types of security personnel—the magical types—who can do all sorts of spells. Like retracing your steps. Or pulling information from your mind without permission."

"A thousand."

"What?"

"A thousand chits." I pulled out one of the blue bars Tom had given me yesterday and placed it on the table in front of the lockbox. "For nothing but a time and a place."

"Holy…" He picked up the bar and ogled it with reverence. "Where'd you even get this?"

I blinked at him. Twice.

"Okay, big secret. Got it." He ran his thumb across the bar and bit down on his lip. "Throw in five hundred more, and I'll whisper the info in your ear, exactly once. But if this blows back on me, I'm breaking into your house, stealing all your shit, and moving to Memphis before I get strung up in a public park."

"Deal." I tucked my fingers behind my ear. "Let's have it."

He brought his mouth close to my ear and mumbled the address of a warehouse, plus a start time of eleven o'clock—tonight. I'd have to come up with a plan of "attack" this afternoon then. Unless I wanted to wait the better part of a week for the next auction to come around. Which would involve me bribing Mo yet again in what was becoming a tedious cycle of monetary exchanges between us.

As I dug around in my pockets for my chit bag to hand

over the promised five hundred, I said, "You going to be there?"

He pulled away from me and held out his hand for the extra chits. "Nah. I got a gig with Joe Shark down on Pulley tonight. He pays better than those auction people, which is ironic considering he doesn't make half of what they do."

Joe Shark was a small-time mob guy who had some very niche lines of business. He owned a couple restaurants and bars that washed his dirty money and acted as fronts for backroom gambling rings. He was fairly harmless, as far as organized crime bosses went.

I counted out the chits from my bag and dropped them onto Mo's open palm. "Well, you have fun. And don't get yourself shot. Or set on fire, again."

His blush returned with a vengeance. "Low blow, man. That wasn't my fault."

I chuckled. "It's always your fault, Mo. You—"

"Freeze! Police," a stern voice called out from the sidewalk.

Men and women dressed in navy blue flooded the court-yard, all of them armed to the teeth with handguns, shock batons, and magic-suppressing handcuffs. There were ten of them in total, each wearing a slightly different expression of anxiety, and they SWAT-shuffled around both sides of the fountain, guns at the ready, to make sure the people at the back of the courtyard couldn't flee through the gate.

All the refugees checking out Mo's wares immediately dropped into huddled balls at the sight of the cops. Several of them whimpered in ways that told me they'd been the victims of military and police brutality during the purge. Mo, on the other hand, stood like a statue, mouth stuck open in shock. He'd never been raided before.

As for me? I just stared at the cops with one eyebrow arched, unimpressed.

What a sloppy entrance. Even a regular human could've escaped nine different ways.

The cops surrounded Mo's tables in a tight half-circle, and I made a three-quarter turn to face the guy who'd stepped a few inches closer than everyone else, assuming he was the leader. The guy was about thirty, and I didn't recognize him from my years on the force. Which meant he was either fresh off the recently rebuilt academy line, or a "transfer," having been a cop in some other city before the collapse. My money was on the latter, based on his age and the way he held himself. He had that rock-rigid posture short men in charge always used to make themselves seem more imposing.

"Hands up where I can see them," he barked at Mo and me.

Mo raised his hands above his head.

I stuck my hands in my pockets, dropping off my chit bag in its usual place, and replied, "Why?"

That threw the cop for a loop. "What do you mean 'why'? I…You're supposed to…" He shook himself out of his confusion and painted the angry face back on. "Enough BS. Put your hands up."

"Am I under arrest?" I drawled. "What am I being charged with?"

He growled at me. Like a tiny dog. "You're not under arrest. We're searching the premises for contraband material, and everyone here is required to keep their hands where I can see them until we're finished. Else we'll bring you in for obstructing an investigation. How's that sound, pal?"

"Where's the warrant?" I pointed at Mo. "You're supposed to show him your warrant before you search the place. Legally."

Short Stack apparently had a short fuse, because he muttered a series of nasty insults under his breath then reached for his cuffs. "Okay, wise guy. You think you know a lot about police procedure? I'll show—"

"He knows everything about police procedure," said a chillingly familiar female voice.

My stomach tied itself into eight different knots.

An eleventh cop walked around the fountain and halted next to Short Stack. She looked older than she had last time I'd seen her, crow's feet and frown lines etched into her freckled face, the consequences of seven hard years. But she still had the same warm brown eyes, the same cute dimples, and the same shock of curly red hair that had made her the butt of many jokes back in the day.

Saoirse Daly. My former partner. My former *senior* partner. The woman my foolhardy younger self had been assigned to when I'd made detective, because Saoirse was known for ironing out wrinkles in rookies. She was strict but fair, kind but hard, no nonsense and extremely intelligent.

And our last conversation had ended with me screaming in her face.

Leave me the fuck alone, you stupid human bitch, is how I phrased it.

Saoirse took a step toward me, lips quirked at one end with a distant fondness. "Been a while, Vince."

"Yes," I answered with the flattest tone I could muster, but somehow, I think the shame still came across. "It has."

"Vince?" Short Stack scrunched his nose. "You know this guy, Lieutenant?"

"Lieutenant?" I tilted my head to the side. "You been climbing the ladder, eh?"

"Well, it has been the better part of a decade." She turned her palms outward. "Can't expect a girl to stay in one place forever, can you?"

"No, I don't suppose you can." I ground my heel into the brick beneath my feet. "But—"

"Hold up," interrupted Short Stack. "'Vince' as in Vincent Whelan? The half-faerie guy who used to be a cop?"

All the other cops went deathly still. I panned my head around to check them out. Some I knew. Some I didn't. The former wouldn't meet my eye, because they remembered what happened seven years ago. The latter stared at me in terror, because they didn't want to get on the wrong side of the fae. Funny thing was not a single one, not even Saoirse, understood how much they were really risking by accosting me. They knew I had a fae parent, but they didn't know what *kind* of fae. And that was the important part. That was the big secret I had to keep.

Or else.

"You caught me, slick," I said to Short Stack before turning back to Saoirse. "Who's this hothead?"

Saoirse stifled a smile. "Nolan Kennedy. Our newest detective."

"And you let him lead raids?" I snorted. "You never let me lead a raid when I was a rookie."

Saoirse didn't answer. She set her jaw in that skewed way she did when she was annoyed by something. Which was the only clue I needed. Kennedy had ridden the nepotism train into the precinct, probably on the coattails of a wealthy or otherwise influential relative. There wasn't much in the way of taxes and government funding yet, so the police were paid via private interests, plus a meager dispensation from our dear faerie "leaders" just to keep the force running at a barebones level in case the donations petered out.

Kennedy had been part of a package deal. Extra funds for his placement in a good job on the force. Probably to keep him off the streets and give him something productive to do so he wouldn't blow all his steam off in the wrong places and embarrass his family. That was probably how he'd gotten all his pre-collapse jobs as well. *He's every bit the dumbass he appears to be too, I bet.*

"They're giving you Kinsale's problem children now?" I asked Saoirse. "Seems a tad unfair, considering the state of things. You don't need any more trouble than you already have."

"Excuse me?" Kennedy snapped. "You don't get to talk about me like that."

I gave him the coldest look I could without dropping my glamours. "Why not?"

He staggered back a step. Then he funneled his fear into more rage and barked, "No more fucking games. I don't care who you are. We're searching this so-called business, and you're either going to submit to a search as well, or we're going to take you to the precinct for questioning regarding reported illicit activity at this establishment."

"Reported?" That pinged my suspicion meter. I shifted my attention to Saoirse. "Why'd you decide to raid Mo's now?"

"Hey," Kennedy said, inching forward, hand tightening on his gun, "*I* was talking to you."

Saoirse ignored him and answered, "We received a package of evidence suggesting this place was part of a drug ring we've been targeting."

Mo, who'd been standing beside me like an ice sculpture

this whole time, whispered so only I could hear him, "No delivery yet today. I'm clear."

"Who sent you this package?" I asked.

Saoirse drew her lips into a thin line. "It was anonymous."

"I bet—"

Kennedy lunged for me, cuffs in one hand, the other outstretched like a claw, aiming for my arm. I dodged to the left, maneuvered around him in a tight arc, swept my foot into both his ankles, grabbed him by the arm, and yanked him sideways without even using any nonhuman strength. Kennedy's knees hit the rim of the fountain basin, and he tumbled face first into a foot of tepid water filled with green slime and dead bugs. He struggled for a few seconds to find purchase against the slippery base, then tore his head out of the water, spitting and gasping.

"You bastard!" he said between wet coughs. "You're under arrest for assaulting a police officer."

"No, I'm not." I shifted toward Saoirse, who was cringing in a way that implied she was calculating how much ass-kissing she was going to have to do to get Kennedy's family to calm down after they found out a group of ten cops had allowed a half-fae to humiliate him in public. I sorta-kinda felt guilty about putting her in that position. But at the same time, the Kinsale PD, at an organizational level, could go hang themselves and strangle to death. Their PR problems weren't my problems. Not anymore. Not ever again.

I cleared my throat to get Saoirse's attention. "I want to see this evidence package."

Saoirse started. "But Vince, it's at the precinct."

"Then I'll go there." I gestured to Kennedy, who was still trying to extract himself from the muck. "Aren't you supposed to bring me in for questioning anyway, since I failed to comply with the terms of your search warrant?"

She opened and closed her mouth several times before she murmured, "You're okay with going to the precinct? After what happened...that day?"

"Not at all. But something about this whole raid scenario feels off to me, and the possibility of 'funny business' is way more important than my personal feelings." I made to move past Saoirse and around the fountain, toward the open gate at the end of the courtyard. No one tried to stop me. "Also, every old-guard cop in the place will be *super* uncomfortable when they see me, and I take no greater pleasure than rubbing someone's nose in their own mess."

CHAPTER SIX

THE PRECINCT HADN'T CHANGED A WHOLE LOT SINCE I LEFT the force. It was the same grungy three-story building on the corner of Bordeo and Planter, an old redbrick structure that had been cracked and stained long before the war broke out. I'd walked the twelve blocks here with Saoirse hanging just behind me, the two of us having left Kennedy and his lackeys to hassle Mo back at the courtyard. Mo would be fine, as long as he really didn't have drugs stashed in his merchandise somewhere. If he did though, that was on him. Drugs were a nasty trade, and I wouldn't bail him out if he got caught with a hand in the cocaine jar.

Saoirse hadn't said anything to me during the entire trip, but I could feel her eyes boring into my neck as I cut through the side parking lot and headed toward the door that all cops used to enter the building when they first got in for their shifts. Admittedly, I should've used the front entrance, like a good little civilian, but I wasn't in a polite or forgiving mood right now. Not after Kennedy made a grab for me. And not after Saoirse told me about this mysterious evidence package that had been dropped on the precinct's doorstep at an extremely convenient time.

When I was a few steps from the door, Saoirse caught up to me and pulled a thin metal plate from her pocket that was fashioned like an ID card. "We have these magic scanners now," she clarified, "instead of an electronic chip system, because the power grid is still spotty and we don't have fuel for our generators." She pressed her card against a section of the brick wall that lined up with the door handle, overtop a black circle that someone had spray painted there. A soft blue glow enveloped the card for a moment, and as it faded, the door unlocked with a series of loud clicks. Saoirse then pulled it open and motioned for me to follow her in. "Evidence room is still in the basement."

The interior of the precinct was in a worse state than the exterior. Not a shocker. At one point during the purge, on the night of a full moon, a pack of nine werewolves had broken into the precinct and trashed the place. Four cops on the night shift had been viciously killed, and two more seriously injured. Yet another had been infected by contact with a wolf's blood and was booted off the force a month later when he himself transformed into a werewolf.

Most of the attackers had been caught in the ensuing weeks—and likely killed when the purge ramped up in the months before the war—but even so, it seemed the wolves had gotten the last laugh.

Seven years on, the walls and floor tiles were still scored with claw marks, and while the glass from broken office and door windows had long been swept away, the panes hadn't been replaced. The holes were covered with what looked to be several layers of butcher paper held in place with gray duct tape. A great deal of the furniture we passed as Saoirse led me to the central staircase was the same stuff that had been there the night of the break-in. The chair cushions were torn. The desks were scuffed. The filing cabinets were dented.

The Kinsale PD might've had an operating budget, but they weren't running on a surplus.

To get to the staircase, Saoirse had no choice but to cut through the main room of the first floor, which contained several groupings of desks assigned to various detective teams. When we first walked into view, everyone in the room was either working diligently or pretending to—a couple were obviously reading books tucked inside manila folders. But Saoirse was such a recognizable person, thanks to her hair, that she caught the eyes of several people, who raised their heads to greet her. And that's when they saw me.

The resulting series of hushed gasps alerted everyone else.

Nobody said a word to me. They just gawked. Until Saoirse and I reached the stairwell and slipped inside. As the door was closing behind us, an epidemic of whispers broke out in the room. A dozen veteran detectives wondering if they'd seen a ghost, and worse, if their past actions (or lack thereof) were finally coming back to haunt them.

If I'd wanted to rattle them even more, I could've told them that it wouldn't be *me* who exacted vengeance on them for their old misdeeds, were the truth about that matter ever to leak to the general public. But I decided to be the better person and keep them in the dark. Even if that was a kindness they didn't deserve.

(I prided myself on not being *quite* as vindictive as my full-blooded faerie relatives.)

The evidence room hadn't changed a great deal either. The barred window that separated the large room full of cardboard boxes from the waiting area now had a few wards drawn onto it in what appeared to be black permanent marker, but I couldn't tell how much juice they had without stripping away my third glamour. Saoirse sauntered right up to the window, rapped on it, and didn't get blasted across the room though, so I figured they weren't too dangerous. Probably just a few defensive measures to prevent theft.

Another old face walked up to the window. Larry Bates, who'd been working the evidence room even when I was a young beat cop. He smiled at Saoirse and opened his mouth to say hello, then he spotted me standing behind her and went white as a sheet. Larry hadn't been involved in the festivities of that fateful day I left the force, but he had been on duty, which meant he heard about it, possibly as it was happening, and had kept his head down so he didn't get the shaft. I didn't entirely blame him for that, but I didn't entirely not blame him either.

I tipped up my chin. "What's happening, Larry? How you been?"

Larry's lips pulled a solid impression of a fish for a few seconds before he found his voice. "Not too bad compared to most, Vince. Wife and kids are okay. Still living in the same house."

"Good to hear. Send Julia my regards."

He put up a smile that so poorly hid his discomfort I was surprised he didn't burst into tears at the effort. "I'll do that."

"Sure you will."

Somehow, Larry paled even more.

Saoirse held one hand behind her back and signaled for me to cut it out, something she'd done in the old days when my mouth ran a bit too fast. She had no authority over me anymore, but I stopped talking anyway, because if I pushed Larry too hard, the resulting breakdown might prevent him from retrieving the papers I needed to examine. And I didn't want this detour to a place filled with my most painful memories to end up a bust. It was already taking every ounce of effort I had not to have a repeat of this morning's bathroom mirror fiasco.

"Larry," Saoirse said, "we need the package on Mo Nielson that came in this morning."

Larry jumped at the sound of her voice. "Y-Yeah, I'll go grab it." He raced away from the window at a speed I was surprised he could reach, and shortly after, the sounds of moving boxes filtered through the gap at the bottom of the window. Larry returned about four minutes later with a box that had NIELSON PACK / ANON written on it, followed by today's date. Larry grabbed the clipboard on the countertop and slid it through the gap. "Just sign for it first, Lieutenant."

Saoirse slipped the pen from under the clip and scrawled her signature. Larry handed over the box and reclaimed his clipboard, watching anxiously as Saoirse and I moved to a small table in the corner of the room. Saoirse sat the box on the table and yanked the top off, revealing a large yellow envelope stuffed with papers. She lifted it from the box and flipped the flap up, then slid the entire stack of papers out, holding them so we could both view the contents.

"These came in via courier this morning," she said. "Mo Nielson's sales records for cocaine and heroin dating back four months, plus several photos of him buying drugs from a known distributor. We've been trying to link him to the drug ring operated by King Keller for six months but had yet to catch him in the act of moving product or obtain definitive evidence that drugs are a part of his bottom line. Until today."

I took the papers from her and leafed through them, skimming for info using a study method Saoirse had taught me during my first year as a detective. The evidence here was pretty damning—I took it back; Mo *wouldn't* be fine—particularly the pictures, which had been taken with a 35mm camera, using actual film developed the old-fashioned way. (Amazing how outdated technology suddenly became relevant again when you had no functioning power grid.) Someone had been keeping tabs on Mo for months, probably one of the organized crime rings he was involved with, in order to build a portfolio of evidence to be used against him if he ever needed to be removed from the game board.

And they chose today, of all days, to cut him loose?

Yeah, no. Coincidences like that didn't happen in the age of magic.

"Okay," Saoirse said, "I've been quiet for long enough. What's all this about, Vince? You think something smells with this package?"

"The package itself? No." I fingered the charm for my third glamour through the fabric of my shirt and quickly whispered the words to dispel it. My magic rose to the surface, a subtle vibration underneath my skin. "The timing of the delivery, yes. I think someone was trying to stop me from talking to Mo, because he's my only contact in the mob world."

Saoirse frowned. "Why do you need a mob contact?"

"New job came in. A little different from my usual fare." I focused intently on the stack of papers and directed a few wisps of my energy into the pages, seeking out any traces of someone else's magic touch. Something in the middle of the stack, a bundle of latent spells, roughly pushed back against the intrusion of my power. I built a little ward wall around it, stifling its ability to counteract me, making sure it didn't follow the trails of my energy as I wove them through all the pages and photos. "I'm guessing somebody followed my new client to my shop and realized they needed to preempt my search for the item I've been charged to find."

My theory was that the auction organizers had told their bosses about Tom's attempt to bribe a look at the buyer list, and said bosses put a tail on him to make sure he didn't keep pushing—or rectify the situation if he did. Of course, he kept on trucking, and now Mo had gotten swept into the consequences of Tom's obsession to find his aunt's long-lost harp of sentimental doom. Mo would be doing time, thanks to this abundance of evidence, and there wasn't much *I* could do for the whiny weasel, other than flip off the people who'd built a blackmail package to hang around his neck.

Looks like I need to befriend a new mob contact.

Oh well.

I didn't find any other signs of foreign magic energy, so I rifled through the stack until I reached the page with the spell bundle embedded in it. I slipped that page out and sat it on the corner of the table farthest away from Saoirse and me, which required me to bend over at an awkward angle, ass sticking straight up in the air. My old partner looked at me like she wasn't sure I was a hundred percent sane. Now, I *wasn't* a hundred percent sane, but no one was these days. So she didn't get to judge.

"You'll see why I did that in a minute," I promised.

Next, I placed the palm of my right hand flat against the top paper on the stack and closed my eyes. Using the threads I'd placed throughout the pages, I encapsulated the entire stack in a spell matrix with a mental push. Then I started speaking. The spell was a long string of complicated words in a language that didn't exist on Earth, and I'm sure it seemed to Saoirse and Larry that I was speaking in tongues. But the instant the last syllable of the last word ghosted over my lips, the trace spell activated with a rush of cold air that billowed out from the stack of papers.

And I was away.

Like an astral projection, I "followed" the papers on their trip to the precinct—in reverse—catching glimpses of buildings and street signs the courier holding the envelope had passed on his way here. Eventually, the regular office buildings and townhouses morphed into warehouses and factories and lots filled with rusting construction equipment. Until the courier walked backward into a particular warehouse, whose main room was totally empty, and then into a small office off that main room. In that office, seated at a desk, was a person—

"Jesus Christ!" Saoirse shouted.

The trace spell collapsed along with my concentration as my eyes popped open to the sight of an aggressively spreading fire on the table in front of me. The spell bundle inside the paper I'd removed from the stack had wormed its way around my stopgap wards and activated upon sensing that someone was using magic on the rest of the pages. It had ignited into a tall flame that was now licking at the ceiling, threatening to catch the entire building on fire.

I tossed the stack of papers back into the cardboard box and held out both my hands toward the billowing fire. I tapped into my magic again, and it was more than happy to comply, as fire was its natural enemy and it wanted to snuff out all the heat in this world. A cold jet of air blasted out of the space between my palms and wrapped around the fire, forming a vortex that siphoned all the oxygen from its center.

The fire fought back, lashing out at me. But the spell bundle had been nothing but a one-off attack with a multistage activation sequence, and its magic energy was limited to what had been stuffed inside the paper. So I kept pushing, strangling it more and more, until it finally gave up the ghost and fizzled out with a bright flash.

A moment later, Saoirse stumbled to a halt beside me, a fire extinguisher in her hand. She stared at the blackened surface of the table, curls of smoke still rising from the char. Then she lowered the extinguisher to her side and sighed. "Way to show me up in my own precinct."

"Your lack of gratefulness implies I should let the evidence room burn down next time."

Her head snapped toward me. "Is there going to be a next time?"

"Not from this stuff." I tapped the rim of the box. "The page I removed a minute ago had a small bundle of 'tripwire' spells embedded in it, so that if anyone tried to use magic to find out who sent the package, it would destroy everything in a big burst of fire, leaving no anchor, which is required for trace spells."

"Is that what you did, a trace spell?"

I nodded.

"Did it work?"

"To a degree." I ran my finger across the burned surface,

leaving a smudge of soot. "I know where it came from, but I only got an incomplete glimpse of the actual sender."

"Where'd it come from?" Saoirse sat the extinguisher on the floor and reclaimed the evidence box, slipping the top back on and tucking it under her arm so it wasn't sitting anywhere near the damaged half of the table. Like she was worried the flame might reignite. "Some mob boss's house?"

"Is that really a question you want to know the answer to?" I flicked the top of the box. "You have a good case against Mo here, and sending him to jail will take a dealer who targets the vulnerable off the street. But if you start asking too many questions about where that evidence package came from, you're going to open a can of worms that could sabotage all the work you've done to clean up this drug ring."

Saoirse shifted her weight from foot to foot, pensive. "You're right, but I feel dirty accepting 'help' from a crime org, particularly when it's a setup to hurt somebody I know and the benefit to the police is just a side effect."

"You got to take the advantages where they come. Because there aren't many these days." I shook my head. "And you don't need to worry about me. I'm going to poke around a bit more and try to figure out why somebody is so hellbent on keeping a damn musical instrument out of its rightful owner's grasp. But if this job gets too dicey, I'll bail. The money is good on this one, but it's not worth my head."

"Wait." Saoirse scrunched her nose in an endearing way that highlighted her freckles. "Did you say 'musical instrument'? This"—she shook the evidence box—"revolves around a musical instrument?"

"Yep. A harp." I couldn't help but smile at her perplexed expression. "Scavengers snatched it. Auctioneers sold it. Rightful owner wants it back. I'm supposed to track the buyer down."

"I don't get it." She wound one of her springy red curls around her finger, something she'd always done when trying to unravel a tangle of clues. "Why go through so much effort to obscure the details of a single auction purchase? Are they that anal about the privacy of their buyers, or is there something more to this harp?"

"Well, it's worth a shit ton of money. But beyond that, who knows?"

Angry yells faintly filtered down the stairs from the ground floor. Kennedy had returned.

"Anyway," I added, "I think I'll take the service stairs out. Unless you want me to *really* embarrass that hothead."

Saoirse rolled her eyes. "I'm sorry about him. He was part of a donation package. Got fired from his old job in Florida for police brutality, *during* the purge."

"Sounds like a bomb waiting to go off. I'd sleep with one eye open, if I were you."

"I've been doing that since I met him."

I started to lift my hand toward Saoirse's shoulder, but couldn't quite push myself to actually touch her in a compassionate manner. It was like there was a wall between us. A wall made of acidic memories, threatening to burn us away if we dared to try and climb it. I could tell that Saoirse felt it too, with the way she glanced at my hovering hand and quickly looked the other way, her hair partially obscuring a grimace, her jaw tensing as she bit her tongue to stop herself from saying something she'd regret.

The stairwell door on the first floor banged open, and somebody came stomping down like a horse.

I faked a cough. "It was, uh, nice seeing you again, partner. Take care of yourself."

Saoirse gathered all the strength she had to look me in the eye, throw on the cheeky grin I'd once loved, and say, "I always take care of myself. You're the one who needs a caretaker, rookie."

Fond memories threatened to break free from the shadows where I'd locked them away, and it was all I could do to say, "See you around, Saoirse." Then I marched across the evidence room, gave a little parting wave to Larry, and slipped into the side hall that led to the service stairs mere seconds before Kennedy stormed out from the main stairwell, huffing and puffing and threatening to blow the entire precinct down.

What was I thinking, coming here after seven goddamn years?
I really was a glutton for punishment, wasn't I?

CHAPTER SEVEN

THE WAREHOUSE I'D OBSERVED DURING THE TRACE APPEARED to be empty when I arrived. As I searched the perimeter for any hidden wards or hiding hostiles, I finished the last few bites of a sub I'd bought on the walk over, crinkled up the paper wrapper, and tossed it onto the overflow pile of a trashcan that hadn't been emptied in about two years. At the sound of the balled-up paper smacking the pile and rolling away, nothing potentially dangerous jumped out at me, in the literal or metaphorical sense. So I stepped off the sidewalk and sidled up to a rusted hole in the chain-link fence just big enough for a man my size to slip through.

I climbed through carefully, making sure the jagged metal didn't graze my skin. On the other side, I paused and again searched the gravel lot for any booby traps, of the mundane or magic sort, but I still didn't find anything that might try to blow me to smithereens. A pinch of suspicion tickling my nose, I continued toward a small side door whose chain and padlock combo appeared to have been broken recently. The metal bits were still lying on the short set of steps leading up to the door. Someone had commandeered the place in the past few weeks. Presumably for "business."

The door opened with no more than a gentle tug, and the hinges, which should have been rusty after years of disuse, were well oiled and soundless. I peeked in to view the shadowy interior of the warehouse. The floor was mostly empty, the inventory having been cleared years back. But there were a few wooden crates atop pallets in one corner that looked pretty new, and fresh scuff marks on the floor indicated they'd been dragged there from the loading dock not too long ago. So the warehouse *was* in use. But who was using it?

And why are they so testy about the harp?

Nothing moved inside the building, so I slipped in and closed the door quietly. I inched along the walls, staying in the darkest shadows, avoiding the dim light cast through the dirty window cut into the roof, until I got close to the office where the courier had received the package. No lights of any kind were on, and the door was closed, which told me the room was unoccupied. But I figured if the place was frequently used as a drop-off point for illicit shipments, there might be records stored in the office. Records containing incriminating information about who ran this operation.

Depending on who that show runner was, I would either continue to search for the harp, or bail out immediately. Some mob bosses in this town were what you'd call "cutthroat bitches," and I wouldn't cross them without a good reason. (Money, for the record, was not a good reason.) The fact that one of them had been willing *to* sacrifice Mo—and that they had known to sacrifice Mo, which meant they knew some key info about me—just to throw me off the harp's trail was a foreboding sign. So if I got confirmation here that the person who sponsored the harp's sale was exceedingly dangerous, I would quit this job in a heartbeat.

I crept over to the office door and reached for the knob, only for my fingers to instinctively pause an inch from touching the metal. My skin prickled with a faint, resonating hum of magic. I took a step back and thoroughly examined the knob, the door, and the frame. It took about two minutes of staring intently, to the point my eyes started to sting, before I picked up hints of wards shallowly etched into the doorframe that had been hidden with extra layers of white paint. Even after I found the spells though, I had trouble keeping track of the energy threads circulating through the ward lines. This was a sophisticated magic security system.

Yet another bad sign.

Because I was fairly certain a brute-force approach would either blow me up, raise a magical alarm, or both, I spent forty-seven minutes dismantling the wards, and suppressing the components I couldn't dispel without alerting the caster. The entire time, I kept looking over my shoulder, at the door I'd used to enter, at the loading bay, whose metal roller doors were down and locked in place, and at every speck of dust stirred by the weak air currents in the building. I hadn't been this paranoid since I went into hiding, after my catastrophic last day on the force, to weather the rest of the purge.

But then, I hadn't broken into a mobster's warehouse before either.

Finally, I rendered the door safe enough to open, and entered the little office. It consisted of a flimsy desk, a chair with a taped-over cushion, and a standard gray filing cabinet. There was a computer on the desk, and it was plugged into the wall, but a quick push of the start button confirmed there was no electricity running to the warehouse. Whoever used this office now hadn't bothered to remove the stuff left behind by the people who'd worked here before the collapse. Or maybe they were just optimistic and thought the lights might come back on sooner rather than later.

Regardless, I ignored the computer and scooted over to the filing cabinet. A quick but thorough check told me it wasn't warded like the door. Which was nice, because I didn't want to waste another hour cracking wards. Only issue was there were no labels on the drawers, and the cabinet had eight drawers. So depending on the filing system, it could still take me a while to sort through the records. Suppressing a sigh, I opened the top left drawer and peered inside.

A tightly packed sea of manila folders. Why was I not surprised?

I tugged out the first folder and held it close to my face so I could read the label inside the green-colored tab on the end of the folder. But the writing turned out to be an abbreviation I didn't know, and a cursory scan of the rest of the folders in the lineup, some of which had green tabs, some yellow, and one red, informed me they all used the same system. So I'd have to actually read the contents of each folder to...*Hold up. They must have a quick way to identify the most important shipping records, right?* I dragged my gaze over the folders again. The colored tabs were the only things besides the actual labels that set them apart. *Could it be that simple?*

Opening the green-tabbed folder in my hand, I skimmed the handwritten cover page of what turned out to be a manifest

for winter coats. Next, I plucked a yellow-tabbed folder from
the middle of the drawer; it contained a manifest for hunting
rifles. Finally, I grabbed the sole red-tabbed folder near the
back of the drawer, flipped it open, and skimmed the summary on the first page. It explicitly used the words "high priority"
and "take utmost care" to describe the shipping strategy for a
million-dollar painting that had been scavenged from a mu-
seum forty miles outside Kinsale.

Bingo.

The red-tabbed folders were for expensive, unique, and
hard-to-acquire items being smuggled into the city. Like the
harp.

Over the next five minutes, I searched every drawer and
pulled all the red-tabbed folders. There were only seventeen,
so I quickly flipped through them, read the cover pages, and
tossed aside any folder that wasn't relevant. When I didn't
find the harp among the three "H" designations on the labels, an itch of irritation started to build in my brain at the
idea the harp may not have even come through here, that
this whole trip was a waste of time. But then, as I opened the
last folder with so much force I tore the spine, I was greeted
by a message in red ink that read: TOP PRIORITY / #TDD4754
/ HARP.

Underneath that header was a description of the harp,
where it had been found—Adelaide, as Tom had said—how it
had been smuggled into the city, and where it was going after
it arrived in this warehouse. Oddly, it had been scheduled to
go to auction *next* week at the time this summary was written.
Something must have changed after the harp departed this
warehouse and got shipped to wherever the auction organizers
stored items slated to go on sale in the near future. But what?

A happenstance reshuffle of the auction schedule? Or something less coincidental?

The summary for this manifest was longer than the others, and it continued onto the back of the cover page. I turned the page over to read the last few sentences, which concerned the condition of the harp and how it had been stored to preserve...

My attention drifted to the bottom of the page. Where a prominent signature had been scrawled in that same red ink. *Agatha Bismarck.*

I dropped the file folder like it was molten rock and recoiled so fast I nearly rammed into the desk. Dread fell over me like a lead-lined blanket, weighing down my every muscle, and the words "oh shit" repeatedly shrieked inside my head. I bit down on my thumb through the fabric of my glove, harder and harder until it started to hurt, until the pain cleared away the panic and I could think clearly enough to devise a plan of escape.

Because I had to get the fuck out of here.

I was standing in Agatha Bismarck's warehouse, searching her private shipping records. And I'd just read definitive proof that the Duchess of Crime herself had personally overseen the recovery and shipment of the harp. That almost certainly meant she'd been the person who approved the rescheduling of the harp's auction slot. And *that* almost certainly meant she'd arranged the harp to be sold to a particular individual under the guise of a normal auction that wouldn't draw the attention of the regular patrons. And Bismarck wouldn't make such arrangements for any old buyer.

Someone very powerful and very wealthy had purchased that harp.

In fact, putting all the clues together, it seemed to me that someone had known exactly where the harp was and asked Bismarck to recover the instrument for them.

No wonder Tom's bribe attempt had been rebuffed. The harp had been a priority item brought into Kinsale to appease someone in the upper crust who had significant dealings in organized crime. Tom's obsession to retrieve it had put Bismarck in an awkward position, because while she might not have minded a lesser buyer's personal information getting bribed out of the ledger, this particular buyer probably valued their privacy a great deal more—and could seriously harm Bismarck's business if they didn't get it.

So Bismarck had sent a tail after Tom, who'd seen Tom recruiting Kinsale's best-known stretch scavenger to locate the harp. Bismarck's lackeys had done a little digging overnight, realized I knew Mo, who occasionally worked at their auctions, and then set Mo up to get arrested so he couldn't give me any information. Unfortunately—for everyone involved, including me—that tactic didn't work thanks to the cops arriving at Mo's about ten minutes too late to prevent our conversation. And because Detective Hothead ticked me off, I was driven to investigate the evidence package Bismarck's people sent out to incriminate Mo. Which led me here.

Crap. I've made a mistake.

One of Bismarck's people would've been watching Mo, and thus already knew the plan had gone awry. That lackey probably switched tactics and started following me after I left Mo's shop. Which meant they saw me go to the precinct—where the evidence package was—and then leave the precinct and walk directly to this secret shipping facility. And in the hour I'd been here, that lackey could've run home and grabbed their friends with the automatic weapons.

Unlike most people, Bismarck didn't fear retaliation from the common paranormals. Hell, she had numerous half-fae working for her, among other nonhumans and human magic practitioners. And since she didn't know what type of fae I was—she likely assumed I had lesser fae blood, because that's what the majority of half-fae had—she wouldn't think twice about ordering her goons to snuff me out. (That would come back to haunt her later, of course, when the powers that be heard she'd made an attempt on my life. But *later* wouldn't help me now.)

Run, Whelan. Fast. Or you're going to end up in a bitch fight.

I couldn't go out the side door because someone would be waiting for me there, so I had to either get past the roller doors and exit through the loading bay or go through the skylight and take the roof option. There was another warehouse about forty feet from the north side of this building, separated by a patch of gravel and the same fence I'd snuck in through. If I took a running leap, and gave myself a magic boost, I could make the jump between rooftops.

The roof option would also lower my chances of getting shot, compared to running at ground level. On the ground, the goons could just spray their guns at me and land a few hits. Shooting up into the air was considerably more dangerous for them, because what went up had to come down. And bullets could come down on your head and brain you.

The roof it was.

I deactivated my first and second glamours with a quick rush of whispered words, sharpening my senses and strengthening my body like I had at Walter Johnson's house. Kicking the stack of file folders out of my path, I swung around to the doorway, eying the skylight above the center of the floor, the invocation for a levitation spell on the tip of my tongue. I stepped out of the office, parted my lips to begin the spell, and—

A huge wooden shipping crate hurtled toward me.

I dropped to my knees, and the crate skimmed my hair, shaving off a few strands, before it crashed into the wall and exploded into a rain of splinters and *silverware*. A few of the splinters nicked my skin—and a fork bounced off my head—but I ignored the pain, heaved myself back to my feet, and spun to the right to find the source of the attack. From a trapdoor cut into the concrete floor, which had been obscured by one of the pallets when I walked by it earlier, men and women in black suits were climbing into the warehouse. Three men were already on the floor, and two of those three were almost eight feet tall and had the bulk to back up their height.

Half-trolls. They had misshapen faces with large, skewed noses, crooked jaws, and bulging eyes, and the seams of their clothing strained to remain intact as they flexed their massive muscles. The one on the right reached for another crate, but the one on the left tapped his shoulder and gave him a hand gesture I interpreted as, "Don't destroy any more of the boss's goods." The half-troll looked miffed he didn't get a second chance to take my head off with a four-hundred pound box.

I glanced up. I wasn't in line with the skylight yet, and the half-trolls could jump high enough to grab me if I didn't quickly shoot up to the roof. So I turned on my toes and dashed toward the faint beam of light cast onto the center of the floor. The half-trolls bellowed in rage and took off after me, their heavy steps vibrating through the floor. The humans around the trapdoor were now pulling out their weapons, an assortment of large-caliber rifles and pistols, preparing to rivet me with a hail of gunfire. Seconds were left on the clock before this devolved into a full-scale battle.

I tried to beat that clock. So hard.

But I didn't make it.

Just as my right foot landed in the square of light, one of the half-trolls lunged for me. He flew twenty feet across the floor so fast he was a blur of writhing muscles and frothing, incoherent shouts. Yelping, I leaped to the side an instant before his meaty fists swung into the space where I had been. He crashed to the floor, cracking the concrete, tearing his suit jacket and shirt clean in half. Then he stood up and casually wiped the debris off, like he hadn't suffered an impact that would've killed a human. He didn't even appear to notice he was bleeding from six places.

The second half-troll had switched directions when I flung myself clear, and as I landed in a smooth slide near the back wall, he barreled toward me, snarling, fist raised to pulverize my head in a single blow. My magic roiled inside my veins, anticipation rising, but I didn't immediately attack. I waited as he drew closer and closer, waited until the huge fist rocketed downward, waited until a self-assured grin of malevolence crawled across the half-troll's face like a wriggling worm. Before I crouched, evading the fist by less than an inch, swung around behind the man, and rammed my magic-infused hand into his back. Then I released the spell I'd been holding on my tongue.

A three-foot-long ice spike formed outward from my fingertips, pierced the half-troll's back, shot out through his abdomen, and rammed into the wall, pinning the man in place. He wailed so loud it hurt my attuned ears and began to viciously thrash, trying to pry himself from the spike. But I'd made it wider at the base so he couldn't easily yank himself free. I had maybe thirty seconds before he managed to break it. Which gave me just enough time to deal with the humans about to shoot me.

I turned on my toes and shot forward, sprinting faster than any human could. The gun-wielding mobsters near the trapdoor were startled by my sudden approach, but they worked with nonhumans all the time, so they didn't let it deter them from taking aim. What deterred them from pulling their triggers, however, was the realization that their half-troll comrade was now directly behind me, pinned to the wall, and he was significantly bigger than me, so if they missed hitting me, they'd hit him instead. One of the women wielding an automatic rifle swore as she flicked her gaze between me and the half-troll.

Then the *other* half-troll came back into play, diving toward me so he could knock me out of alignment. But I'd anticipated that. Because half-trolls were not the smartest lot.

I dropped into a slide that took me underneath the half-troll's hulking form as he soared through the air. His grabbing fingers missed the collar of my coat by a fraction of an inch. My open palm did not miss smacking his stomach, at which point I unleashed yet another spell—that covered him head to toe in four inches of solid ice. Frozen in place, unable to control his trajectory or prep for a landing, the half-troll careened into the office and slammed into the filing cabinet, crumpling the weak metal with a loud, echoing screech.

I sprang back to my feet, raised my other hand toward the group with the guns, and made a punching motion, unleashing the last spell on the roster—the last attack spell I could muster without digging too deeply into my magic and risking its siren song overtaking my judgment. A cold blast of air shot out from my hand, and halfway to the group, a hundred pieces of baseball-sized hail formed at its front.

The humans couldn't move quickly enough to avoid the onslaught. The ice chunks utterly wrecked them. One woman took a piece to the jaw so hard it gave her whiplash. One man's nose imploded with a resounding crack, blood spurting out every which way. The rest suffered broken ribs and arms and legs, bruised and ruptured organs, severed blood vessels and wicked concussions. And some poor fellow took a blow to the groin that I was fairly certain rendered him infertile. When the hailstorm ended, all eight of them were down, and no one had a finger on a trigger.

Somewhere behind me, the half-troll I'd pinned was on the cusp of breaking the ice spike. Off to the right, his buddy was trying to extricate himself from the warped piece of metal that had once been a filing cabinet.

Time to go.

I ground my boots into the concrete and made a sharp turn, bounding toward the square of light. Crossing into it, I slid to a stop in the middle, called up my magic again (and ignored its assertive impulse to *destroy all my enemies*), and funneled energy into my legs. I crouched, took a deep breath, and as both half-trolls were pulling free from my stalling tactics and preparing to make another charge, I launched myself straight up off the floor.

I shot toward the skylight, arms over my head for protection, smashed through the glass, and drifted another ten feet into the air before I started to come back down. With a few whispered words, I caught myself with a swirling air spell, pushed my body out of alignment with the hole where the skylight had been, and lowered myself gently onto the rooftop. Gently being that I acquired less than ten bruises.

From below, the half-trolls roared, and one of them made a jump for the hole. He actually managed to grab onto the frame of the skylight, but the jagged glass left behind by my ascent bit into his fingers, and the slippery blood caused him to lose his tenuous grip. He plummeted back down into the warehouse, and from the rumbling boom of his impact, followed by a furious yell, I guessed he landed right on top of his buddy.

Two birds with one stone. Nice.

I would've loved to look down into the hole and laugh at them. But I wasn't suicidal.

After getting my bearings, I located the other warehouse nearby and took off running for the edge of the roof. One magic-powered long jump later, I was in the clear, no half-trolls in pursuit, no goons with guns firing pot shots at me. My magic was still whipped into a frenzy though, which was irritating, because in that state, it constantly challenged my rationality. But I couldn't bottle it up again. Not yet.

I was a marked man now, and that mark belonged to the Duchess of Crime.

If I wanted to avoid having a bounty put on my head, I was going to have to get that mark removed. At the source.

Fuck you, Tom. You and your stupid harp.

CHAPTER EIGHT

THE FIRST THING I DID AFTER I PUT A WIDE BERTH BETWEEN myself and the warehouse was attempt to call Tom. Now, the cell phone network in Kinsale was about as reliable as the power grid, and my phone was running on a low charge because I hadn't swung by the library to leech off their electricity in over a week, so it took me almost half an hour of checking my signal in various places, including rooftops, before I finally got enough bars to try Tom's number. And then the asshole didn't pick up.

I considered whether his silence meant he'd been snuffed out by Bismarck, but even if he had, there was nothing I could do about it. Bismarck was too rich and influential to get any blowback from ordering a hit on some schmuck, even if that schmuck was well off enough to live in Rosewood. Plus, I wasn't entirely sure Tom didn't deserve to get the axe.

I didn't think it was possible that he'd gone to one of

Bismarck's auctions without realizing who the head honcho was. He'd said himself that he had to "schmooze" the right people to score an invite to one of the auctions sponsored by the organization that had recovered the harp. And if Tom had indeed known Bismarck had been in possession of his harp, then he'd set me up to butt heads with her from the beginning. That forty grand was starting to seem less like the big prize I was promised and more like a pittance meant to lead me to my funeral.

Being tricked really pissed me off.

Stomping my foot on the roof of the shed where I stood, I turned off my phone to conserve what battery power remained and shoved it back into my coat pocket. Then I hopped down onto the wet brown grass and squelched off across the front lawn of an empty house. By the time I reached the sidewalk, the vague outline of a plan to get myself out of this mess was brewing inside my mind. But as I headed for the nearest intersection, I realized none of my viable options were attractive. They all involved tradeoffs that were going to leave me sore for a long, long time.

Ultimately, I decided to go with the most direct approach.

It would hurt more now and less later.

The first step was to find Agatha Bismarck, for which I already had a lead. Bismarck was known to frequent the only fancy sit-down restaurant left in the entire city, which had been funded with her money and employed a bunch of actual chefs she'd plucked from the initial influx of refugees after the city gained its protected status. It was called Raphael's, and it served cuisine that was an approximation of French fine dining, the closest you could get from the food that could be grown during this dreary winter.

She usually stopped in around lunch with a couple of her "accountants" to wash some newly laundered money and have a lovely meal. It was almost lunchtime now, so if I hurried across town, I might get there while she was still eating. She'd have an entourage of personal guards, several of them nonhuman, but I was good enough at veil spells and the basic art of common sense to slip in through one of the restaurant's blind spots and approach her.

My plan was to act like a badass and intimidate her until she agreed to stop hassling me. Depending on her degree of stubbornness, that could involve revealing what type of fae my mother was. Which would suck—but it would also instill the fear of god into Bismarck. Or at least a sense of pragmatism. I didn't know if she actually felt fear. Regardless, Bismarck was smart enough to know she shouldn't mess around with somebody like me. Humans "messing around" with people like me was the reason Washington, DC no longer existed.

So, yeah, I was going to verbally bitch slap the Duchess of Crime.

As far as plans went, it wasn't my best.

But it wasn't my worst either.

When I made it to the edge of downtown, I slowed from a jog to a casual stride that wouldn't make me stand out from the crowd. I continued on around the perimeter of the busy market and onto Pequot Street, which housed some of the better-funded businesses in Kinsale:

A big bank that hadn't changed much since the collapse, other than switching currencies. A hardware store slash actual blacksmith's shop that I avoided like the plague—because *iron*. A clothing boutique run by seamstresses who made their clothes from scratch. And finally, situated in the middle of the street, where everyone could see its sign for half a mile in both directions, was Raphael's.

You couldn't get through the front door if you weren't on a list, and the crowd around the entrance was too big for me to slip through under a veil—veils made you invisible, not intangible. So I snuck around to the alleyway between the restaurant and the office building next door. After checking to ensure I wasn't being watched, I whispered a couple sentences and made a motion with my hands that mimicked throwing a blanket over my head. The world around me dimmed slightly, confirming my veil was active.

Next, I sidled up to the side door and listened closely. I could hear pots and pans clanging in the kitchen, and the murmur of the cooks conversing. I didn't want to have to open the door if it wasn't strictly necessary, because someone would notice a door opening by itself. So I waited a few minutes in the hopes that an employee would walk out for a smoke break or to toss some trash into the nearby dumpster.

I got my wish. Three minutes into my wait, a woman bearing trash bags kicked the door wide open. As soon as she was clear of the threshold, I skirted around her and hurried inside before the door banged shut. I found myself in a dark room full of cleaning supplies that let out into the kitchen.

Shuffling forward, I peered out and scrutinized all the staff working at the various prep and cook stations. None of them stuck out to me as obviously paranormal. When I sent out a very faint ping of magic that didn't extend beyond the kitchen, no one visibly reacted or sought me out with their own magic probe.

The coast was clear.

The trip through the kitchen was fraught with near misses,

because the kitchen staff moved like lightning. Several times, I almost collided with someone who moved unexpectedly. But I made it to the double doors that separated the kitchen from the dining room without giving myself away, and yet again waited for a server to come or go. This time, my cue came around a lot quicker, because Raphael's was bustling. Which wasn't a surprise. There was no other restaurant in the city where rich people could flaunt themselves.

Once in the dining room, I hunkered down in the darkest corner I could find and sought out Bismarck. She wasn't hard to locate. There was a big half-circle booth in the corner opposite where I was standing, and Bismarck was lounging on the plush cushion, sipping a glass of wine and picking at some sugary dessert that had no business being made in a post-apocalyptic society.

The Duchess was about forty-five, but looked considerably younger, with thick, dark hair wound up in a bun, a full complement of makeup that would've cost a fortune *before* the collapse, and vivid green eyes that gave off the impression they could pierce your soul. There was no one in the booth with Bismarck, but her mouth was moving as if she was holding a conversation. My eyes picked out a cell phone sitting on the table next to her plate. She was on a call. And she didn't seem too happy about its subject.

I needed to get closer to hear what she was talking about, because the din of the busy restaurant was too dense to pick out Bismarck's voice from across the room, even with my superhuman hearing. There was, however, a problem with closing the gap between us: the five elf guards who were hanging out at various points in the room. Not half-elves either. These were full-on elves. Whom Bismarck must've paid a fortune. Elves considered working for humans to be a denigrating chore, and needed ample incentive to do it.

Irony was that elves were practically made to be bodyguards for people who had magically inclined enemies. Their tall, willowy builds caused people to underestimate their strength. Their pointy ears could hear far better than my half-fae variety. And their eyes had the power to pierce through illusory magic. Like the veil I was currently wearing. The only reason they hadn't spotted me when I walked into the dining room was because there was a large potted plant with tall fronds sticking up from atop a decorative half-wall that set the seating area apart from the bar, which was situated to the right of the kitchen doors.

Lucky break.

But now I had a real conundrum on my hands. How could I evade detection by the elves long enough to sneak into Bismarck's booth? I mean, sure, I didn't *need* to sneak into her booth, but it would be way more terrifying for Bismarck if I seemingly appeared out of nowhere sitting right next to her. And I really wanted to rattle her after she sent those half-trolls to beat me to a literal pulp.

The answer to my problem turned out to be the equivalent of an adolescent prank. When another server bearing a large tray of food emerged from the kitchen and continued straight toward the far side of the dining room, I ducked down beside him and crawled along on my hands and knees, the half-wall protecting me from those keen elf eyes. At the end of the bar area, where the half-wall ended, the server turned to make the single step down into the dining area. At the perfect moment, as the server had one foot in the air and the other on the edge of the step, I reached out and yanked on the man's pants leg.

The guy lost his footing with a gasp and stumbled forward, his tray tipping over and spilling food onto an occupied table with a series of clatters and clangs and the unmistakable sound of breaking glass.

I rapidly scooted back along the half-wall until I reached the other end, and peered around the edge. All five elves were looking at the dismayed server, the complaining rich people he'd spilled food on, and the general mess on the table and floor, searching for any signs of trouble for Bismarck. Keeping my head low, I crept out from behind the wall and did an awkward squat-shuffle across the dining room, pausing when I fell into the cover of each table, until I reached the back wall and tucked myself in the corner where the row of booths gave way to the restrooms. The elves didn't even glance my way.

Now, I thought, peeking around the last booth in the line-up, *to make the final stretch to Bismarck. Should I go for speed? Another distraction? Some other…?*

I halted my plotting when Bismarck's voice drifted into my ear. Only four booths from her table, and with much of the dining area hushed as they watched the confrontation between the mortified server and the irate patrons, I could hear Bismarck's end of the phone conversation that was still dragging on. My ears also picked up a faint bass coming through the speaker, but I couldn't make out any of the man's words. So I focused on what Bismarck was saying.

"You didn't tell me you would wait so long to cast the harp spell," she hissed into the mic. "Now I've got the sharks circling me, and they're moving in for the kill." She paused while the man on the other end replied. "No, I don't mean literally. They tapped that half-fae stretch scavenger, Whelan, to look into the harp's sale. He was a detective before the collapse, and a damn good one apparently. He's already managed to track the harp back to the warehouse on Morrison Road, and he found the shipping records. He knows there's something off about the sale. We can only hope he hasn't figured out what the harp *is*."

The man said something in an angry tone, words almost loud enough to parse.

Bismarck sighed. "You think I didn't try to stop him? I sent a whole team to 'dissuade' him from continuing to poke around in my business. Now, all those people, good people, are in the hospital, including two of my limited number of half-troll soldiers. And Whelan is in the wind."

The man snapped back, and Bismarck inhaled.

"Handle it how?" she said, more tentative than before. "It's one thing to send people to take care of Whelan in an otherwise abandoned warehouse in a largely empty neighborhood, but he's not there anymore. If he's in a populated area, there's only so much we can do without raising an alarm. If you do anything too public, you're going to have the dullahan swarming us in no time. And then you won't be *able* to wait for tonight's full moon, or that witching hour you're so intent on, because the fae will be ripping you limb from limb."

The man spoke again, calmer this time.

"Really? There exists such a creature?" Bismarck sounded impressed. "I had no clue. But if that's the case, then go ahead and unleash your hound, or whatever. If it takes care of Whelan and doesn't risk exposing your plan for the harp—or my role in it—then we're fine. I just don't want any blowback on my enterprises as a result of this scheme. I went out of my way to get you that harp while keeping it off the radar of the sídhe. I'll lose my head if they connect the dots before you successfully wake your friends from their extended nap. And my death was not part of this deal."

The man said a few final lines in a way that struck me as mollifying, then hung up.

Bismarck spent a few more minutes finishing up her wine and dessert before she snapped her fingers, getting the attention of her guards, and slipped out of the booth. She walked to the front door surrounded by the elves, one of whom opened the door for her, one of whom exited first to scout ahead and ensure no one accosted her. When the latter gave the all clear, Bismarck left the restaurant, and despite the sour look on her face, painted lips pursed, she didn't seem nearly as worried as she should've been about the fact she had wrapped herself up in a conspiracy to challenge the faeries who now ruled the world.

I, on the other hand, was freaking the fuck out.

For almost ten minutes, I remained squatting behind the booth, next to the men's bathroom door, grinding my teeth against a gloved knuckle and resisting the urge to hyperventilate. Up until this moment, I had assumed Tom was simply some idiotic young brat with a deep wallet who intentionally left out some crucial details about his aunt's precious harp and its recent sale in order to convince me to help him get it back. Namely, that it had been sold by Bismarck to an important buyer. But I'd been wrong. So, so wrong. Tom wasn't an idiotic young brat at all. Hell, he probably didn't exist. The guy who showed up at my shop was probably an actor hired for the "Tom role."

I'd been played. Like a goddamn harp.

Someone had intentionally pushed me into a conspiracy—with no way out.

Bismarck was working with a man in Kinsale's paranormal community to cast some kind of powerful spell. I knew it was powerful because no one waited until the witching hour on the night of the full moon to cast weak spells. That was reserved for the "mother of all spells," the kind of spells that only got cast once a century. And this particular spell involved that godforsaken harp, which I now understood was no simple musical instrument. It was a *magical* instrument, presumably one of great effect.

According to that phone call, Bismarck's mystery buyer was planning to wake up a group of paranormal creatures from what I gathered was a magically induced coma. A group that the fae would object to being woken. *This is bad. This is very, very bad.*

What made it worse was that I couldn't just run to the dullahan, or any other fae authority in Kinsale, and tell them what was happening. Because that would bring their wrath down on the city—they didn't give two shits about collateral damage; as long as there were *some* humans left alive, that was good enough for them—and severely damage what little civilization had been rebuilt here since the collapse. The fae always used "the big guns" when they moved against a potentially serious enemy. All that subtle mischievous manipulation endemic to the faerie myths and legends was reserved for when the fae didn't think you could actually harm them.

They liked to tease the weak.

They loved to annihilate the strong.

Squatting in the middle of a busy restaurant full of oblivious rich people who had no clue their city was on the cusp of destruction yet again, I could only curse myself for falling into "Tom's" trap, for letting myself get blinded by the prospect of a fat bank account. I knew that in the world of the fae, anything that seemed too good to be true *always* was. But seven years after the end of the life I'd lived for over two decades, I was still stuck in the mindset that Earth was a human world, and such idiosyncrasies did not apply.

Foolish little half-fae, I spit at myself, *this world doesn't belong to the humans anymore.*

O'Shea was spot on. This was a brave new world. And I wasn't nearly as ready for it as I'd been pretending. Now my lack of preparation had bitten me in the ass so hard I wasn't sure I'd be able to walk out of this situation alive.

I couldn't go to the fae leaders to stop Bismarck's partner. I couldn't go to the cops, because many of them were in Bismarck's pocket, and plus, they hardly had the power to challenge her large supply of nonhuman goons. I couldn't go to my friends, like Christie and O'Shea, because they were only human, and not the soldiering sort, and would end up dead long before I did. I would have to go this one alone, and I would have to drum up the courage to do so now, if there was any hope of stopping Bismarck and her partner from sending another massive quake through this already cracked and broken world.

Sure, I could've chosen to retreat to my store full of shit and keep my head down and let the world burn down around me. Sure, I was tempted to do just that, because in many ways and for many reasons, I hated this world and the people in it. And sure, I had no obligation whatsoever to be the big hero, save the day, and defeat the dastardly villains.

But I chose to try anyway. Because once upon a time, that had been my job. And though I would never admit it out loud, I missed being a detective.

Well, I suppose getting killed by an asshole with a harp is better than getting eaten by ghouls in the stretches. So at least there's one "pro" to pit against a thousand "cons."

Yay?

CHAPTER NINE

I SPENT THE NEXT HALF HOUR WANDERING AIMLESSLY through the crowds of the market, occasionally ducking into tents and discreetly attaching myself to groups of people to better blend in. Bismarck had said something about a "hound" being sent after me, which could refer to any number of paranormal creatures. Hellhounds, for example, were sometimes used like police dogs, to hunt down and subdue fugitives on the run—or to pin your enemies so they couldn't escape. Regardless of what type of paranormal dog it was though, I doubted it could be easily deployed in a heavily populated area. And the central market was the busiest place in town.

While I wandered, I contemplated how to approach the recovery of the harp now that I knew its buyer was a man who commanded considerable magic. If not his own, then the magic of someone under his employ. But after using a fair amount of brain power to tackle the problem from every conceivable direction, I ended up right where I'd started: I needed the buyer's name and address. There was no other way I could track him down. And getting those meant retrieving the auction ledger.

That was a problematic proposal, however, because Bismarck and company would be on high alert after my escape, and she knew that I knew the guy in possession of the harp had bought it via a fixed auction. So she would beef up security, using her elf lackeys, to make sure I couldn't sneak into tonight's auction and snatch the ledger with all the incriminating information inside.

Either that, or she would straight up destroy the page of the ledger that contained the damning info. But I doubted she'd go for that option. Since I hadn't been caught at Raphael's, she had no reason to believe I was sneaky enough to evade her hired elves. And Bismarck was far too proud to admit her operations were vulnerable to a "mere" half-fae without irrefutable proof. I would bet money on the ledger still being intact.

So I decided to stick to my original plan. I would attend the auction and grab the ledger.

Except I now needed a better strategy than waltzing in and taking it while throwing a few puffs of magic to daze and confuse the human mooks. I'd be up against the serious mooks now. The elves. The half-trolls. The human magic practitioners. And whatever else Bismarck had on her payroll. In order for me...

Something growled. Loudly. Behind me.

Which should've been impossible. Because right now, as I stood between a booth selling hot soup and a tent selling rain coats, both of which were booming, nothing large enough to produce a bone-shaking growl would've been able to fit among the throngs of people tromping around me. Unless…A faint childhood memory flitted around the periphery of my mind, teasing me. Unless…What was it? I knew the term. I'd heard of this creature before. I'd seen it before, I was sure. *What the hell is it? What is it called?*

It growled again. Even louder. Even closer.

With immense trepidation, I peered over my shoulder.

And the memory slipped into place with all the grace of a lightning strike.

The "hound" was called a barghest, and to summon one from the Otherworld to Earth required a blood sacrifice and the signing of a magic contract that basically said your soul was forfeit if you were unable to pay an "adequate fee" for the creature's service. On the surface, a barghest was not unlike a hellhound, in that it could track its prey by even the faintest scents and never tired, never slept, never slowed. It was the same color as a hellhound too, black as night with red, glowing eyes, and teeth so sharp they could flay the skin from your muscles.

But there were a few key differences between a barghest and a hellhound. The first was that a barghest was far more intelligent than a hellhound. It was a fully sentient creature with its own will. The second was that a barghest had the quirky ability to be intangible, inaudible, and invisible to all except the contract holder—and the person whose scent it was following. In other words, here in the market, no one but me could see it, no one but me could hear it, and no one but me could touch it. And third, the last difference, and perhaps the most subtle and nuanced difference of them all:

A hellhound was the size of a large dog, and a barghest was the size of a large car.

I made eye contact with the barghest standing ten feet behind me, and involuntarily let out a whimper. In response, the barghest roared like an enraged lion and *pounced*.

And did I run away screaming like a small child?

Yes. Yes, I did.

During my life-or-death sprint through the market, I mowed down about twenty people, ripped straight through the backs of four tents—because the barghest couldn't phase through unattached objects, only living things and the objects in their spiritual fields—left the market, crossed the street, and finally crashed headfirst through the glass door of a small shop selling homemade soap and shampoo.

The customers and employees shrieked as a wall of fragmented glass sailed across the room, but I didn't have time to apologize, because the barghest was seconds behind me. Ignoring a dozen bleeding cuts on my face and neck, I flung myself over the checkout counter, barreled through the door into the employee-only area, and hightailed it down a narrow hall that let out into a wide back alley between two rows of stores. Then I fled down said alley as fast as my legs could take me without ripping the limbs from my body.

The barghest, which was too bulky to fit through the shop's door, had to choose to go over or around. It chose over. It leaped onto the roof, cracking the material beneath its massive paws, raced across, and dove off the back end, landing on the ground about fifty feet behind me. It quickly sighted me again, snarled, and took off, its claws leaving deep gouges in the concrete as it tried to thrust itself forward fast enough to catch me and rip me clean in half with its powerful jaws. And it would've succeeded too, if I hadn't lived in Kinsale for most of my life.

At the very end of this alley was a metal grate that covered an access shaft for the city's underground flood diversion system. Back when I'd been a detective, I'd caught a serial killer in one of the flood tunnels after Saoirse and I figured out the man was using them to sneak into residential neighborhoods unseen during the day, where he could easily abduct children from their yards. As part of our plan to invade the tunnels in force and head the perp off before he could strike again, I'd memorized the locations of most of the entry points to the system.

Including the one right in front of me.

I shot a cold blast of energy at the grate, which sheared through the locks securing it and flipped it open. Then I dropped into an angled slide, ignoring the rough friction of the concrete on my clothing and skin, and slipped over the lip of the hole that dropped off into absolute darkness. My body sensed the ground approaching before I could see it, so I righted myself and splashed down into about six inches of water, what remained of yesterday's storm.

Above me, the barghest skidded to a stop in front of the opening and peered down, growling and spitting at me, shoving its head through the gap and snapping its jaws. I waved at it and said, "Better luck next time."

Then I ran away again. Because barghests were scary.

About a mile later, I came to a halt at an intersection that was a good distance away from any points of egress. It was impossible to escape from a barghest indefinitely, as it could pick up even the faintest scent using its preternaturally powerful nose. But as long as the creature couldn't *get* to me, I was safe. Now if only I could live in the tunnels beneath Kinsale forever, with no food or other supplies. And if only I didn't have to get the ledger from tonight's auction. And if only I didn't have less than twelve hours to stop someone from casting a spell with precarious aftereffects.

I paced back and forth, kicking up water in frustration, as I tried to figure out what to do. The barghest would catch up to me again if I spent too much time trying to infiltrate the auction, and the location of tonight's auction was nearly half a mile from a tunnel entry point. If I unleashed my full power, I might be able to kill it, but not without causing a massive ruckus that would alert every cop, mobster, and nosy citizen in town. Plus, I hadn't released my fifth and sixth glamours in almost twenty years, and the last time I'd done so, it had been to…less-than-stable results.

My faerie side got a tad manic after being cooped up behind so many glamours for years on end.

No, I needed a better plan than a slugfest with the barghest.

More than that, I needed *help*.

The mere idea left a bad taste in my mouth. During the purge, asking for help, from either humans or other paranormals, had meant putting them on the chopping block with you, if you were caught by the military or the militarized police who'd prowled the streets. Since that was the sort of guilt that would gnaw at your heart, most people who were purge targets learned to fend for themselves. They learned how to hide, how to gather supplies without being noticed, how to keep their families and friends safe from persecution.

It had been almost seven years since the purge ended, but old habits died hard.

Although, if I was being honest, my biggest problem was *who* I had to call for help. Because, again, I couldn't just drag O'Shea or Christie or some other noncombatant into this mess, and there was only one person with significant combat experience *and* undercover experience who I knew would help me if I asked. There was no contest, nothing to debate. I had to call her. Yet I still spent a whole ten minutes biting my thumbnail bloody before I finally had the guts to pull my cell phone from my pocket and find the right number in my contacts.

Bafflingly, my cell phone had nearly full bars right now. *All that time I spent waving the damn thing around on rooftops, when I could've stuck it down a sewer drain. Stupid cell network. Stupid...* I shook my head. *Stop stalling and hit the call button, you coward.*

My thumb hovered over the green button.

Do it!

I pressed the button and held the phone to my ear.

She answered on the second ring. "Lieutenant Daly, Kinsale PD."

I took a stilted breath and replied, "Hey, Saoirse. Guess who?"

"Vince?" she said quietly, sounding alarmed. "What are you calling me for?"

"What? I can't call my old partner for a chat?"

"Of course you *can*, but you haven't." The sound of a chair rolling on worn wheels came across the line. "You hadn't spoken to me for seven years until this morning, and now you're casually calling me on the phone?"

"Or not so casually." I injected an ounce of exasperation into my voice. "I'm in a bit of a pickle."

"The last time you said that to me"—her voice dropped an octave—"was just before you got kidnapped by the leader of a drug cartel. So what the hell have you gotten yourself into this time?"

I sighed. "I'm being chased by a paranormal dog the size of a Ford F-150 because someone is trying to prevent me from saving the city from disaster." Saoirse inhaled sharply and started to respond, but I cut her off and continued, "And that's all I'm going to tell you over the phone. Because people could be listening in, using a variety of spells, or a variety of totally mundane spying equipment."

"Vince," she said. "I swear, if you're going to tell me I can't—"

"You can't say anything to any of the other cops. They could be on the payroll of somebody involved on the wrong side of this mess."

Something clunked on her end. I thought it might've been her head smacking her desk. "You're going to be the death of me."

"If you agree to help me, that is not out of the realm of possibility."

"Jeez, you really know how to entice a girl."

"That particular skill has never been in my repertoire, as you well know."

"For the love of…" She groaned. "All right, fine. I'll *listen* to your explanation of this zany situation you've tangled yourself up in, and then I'll make a decision on whether or not to 'participate' in whatever perilous role you've got planned for me. I assume you want to meet in some clandestine location?"

"You think right."

"Where?"

"Well, you remember that case with Frankie Dillinger, the child killer?"

Silence. For a literal two minutes. And then, "You don't mean you want to meet in the…"

"I'm already there."

"Oh, fuck me." Her chair flew back on squeaky wheels and slammed into something. "I'm going to need my rain boots, aren't I?"

I stared at the half foot of water soaking my pants. "That would be advisable."

CHAPTER TEN

Saoirse and I rendezvoused in the tunnel where I'd once tackled a serial killer, and neither of us were happy about it.

The barghest had tracked me down again when I was halfway to my destination, sniffing my scent out even through the deep earth that separated me from the surface. I'd had to take a roundabout path through the tunnels, and shed several pieces of my clothing, letting them float away atop the rushing water, in order to confuse the creature's tracking and get it off my tail. If it found me while I was talking to Saoirse, she could end up a target as well, depending on what orders the barghest's summoner had given it.

The source of Saoirse's irritation was more mundane than mine: She'd slipped at some point while walking through the tunnels and fallen flat on her ass, and she was soaked from the hips down, her rain boots full of water. When she caught me in the beam of her flashlight, leaning against the wall, missing my belt, both socks, and the tie I usually wore to look "professional," she huffed angrily and squelched over to me. The moment she reached spitting distance, she said, "Next time, I get to pick the location of our secret meeting."

"You're a lot more optimistic than me if you think there's going to be a next time."

She rolled her eyes. "Enough with the apocalyptic cynicism. We've been there. We've done that. The nuclear war already happened." She deliberately shined the flashlight into my eyes. "Tell me what nonsense is happening now."

I squinted and pushed the flashlight away. "Honestly, I don't know all the details yet, but..." I recounted everything from my meeting with Tom up until the point where the mystery buyer's barghest found me and chased me through the market. "And that's how I ended up hiding in these dark, wet tunnels, slowly getting poisoned by mold inhalation."

Saoirse paced around in a circle as she processed my words, sloshing water to and fro. After another lengthy silence, she said, "Leave it to you to get chased by the most ridiculous monsters."

"That's a feature, not a bug," I replied.

"A feature of *what?*"

"Being half fae."

She stopped pacing. "What do you mean?"

"Well, if I was human, do you really think this buyer would've used dangerous blood magic to summon a creature from the Otherworld to hunt me down and kill me?" I raised my arms in an exaggerated shrug. "My guess is no. He probably would've hired a hitman to snipe me with a high-powered rifle from a distance. Or, were I a magic practitioner, a practitioner hitman to snipe me with a high-powered spell from a distance."

"So the ridiculousness of the tool used to kill someone is proportionate to how much nonhuman blood they have. Is that what you're saying?"

"Not so much ridiculousness as effectiveness." I dropped my hands and tucked them into my coat pockets. "Barghests are determined bastards, even when they're not being driven by a blood contract. That thing's not going to leave me alone until its master either dissolves the contract, which could mean forfeiting his own life, depending on the terms, or gets killed some other way."

"You're in real danger then." Saoirse drew her brows together, troubled. "Can the dog monster be killed?"

"Everything can be killed, even the so-called immortals." I pulled away from the wall and let out a frigid white breath into the humid air. My unglamoured magic was still bugging me, a low buzz deep in my bones. It was vexed I hadn't used it to wrestle with the barghest and had instead fled like a wimp. "The real question is 'Can *I* kill it?' and the answer is, 'I'm not sure.' Maybe if I go all out, but that's a dangerous proposition in and of itself."

Saoirse eyed my breath in the air. Hers wasn't turning white. "I'm not sure what 'go all out' entails for a half-fae. Does that have something to do with, uh, what's it called? A glamour? The magic mask thing you use to look more human?"

"Glamours are a tad more complex than masks. But you're on the right track." I reached under my shirt collar and tugged out my necklace, shaking it to jangle the charms. "Half-fae like me have six glamours. Each one conceals a different part of my faerie side. Usually, when I get into a fight that requires more than human ability, I strip off glamours one, two, and three, which correspond to senses, physical performance, and magic energy. I never drop four, five, and six, however, because those cause more…fundamental alterations to my person."

Saoirse tugged on a damp curl of hair. "But if you did drop those, you would gain enough power to defeat the barghest?"

Definitely. "Perhaps."

"Hm." She tapped her thumb against her flashlight. "But if glamour three gives you access to your magic, why is that not enough to fight the barghest on its own?"

Ah, Saoirse. Always so perceptive.

"Because faerie magic isn't human magic. My ability to use magic is limited, even with my energy technically available, as long as my three base glamours are intact."

"Interesting." She skewed her lips to the side, a sign that she was making a mental note to do more research on this topic later. Which was not something I wanted her to do, but arguing with her about it was pointless. Saoirse went wherever the clues led her, an aspect of her personality that applied to her personal life as well as her professional one. Some people called her nosy for it, but I'd once thought it an endearing trait. Then the purge started and anyone who got outed as a paranormal ended up on the government's kill list.

The possibility of my own partner finding out what I was became considerably more unnerving after that. (Though in the end, it *wasn't* Saoirse who found me out.)

"Okay," she finally said, "let's leave you unleashing your full power to kill the dog monster as the last-ditch option. We'll first aim for capturing—and perhaps killing, if it comes to that—this partner of Bismarck's who wants to cast the threatening spell tonight."

"You're all right with working off the books, *Lieutenant?*" I asked, genuinely curious. Saoirse had been a stickler for the rules back in the day. I had continually exasperated her by ever so slightly bending them whenever I had the opportunity.

Hey, I was part faerie.

That's how we rolled.

Saoirse swept up her foot and sent a wave of water at me, drenching my pants legs yet again. "Oh please. 'Off the books'? There *are* no books, Vince. You know as well as I do that the police are just following the equivalent of a taped-up instruction manual someone dug out of the trash. We have no constitution to follow, for god's sake, much less a set of criminal laws, or judicial precedents, or even an approved set of procedures and regulations. All that went out the door when the great Queen Mab snapped her fingers and wiped DC off the face of the Earth."

I roughly cleared my throat. "Don't say her name out loud. Not here. Not now."

Saoirse cocked an eyebrow. "Why? You hate her too?"

"While I do indeed despise that woman with all the fury in my frozen half-fae heart, that is not the reason you shouldn't say her name out loud," I answered. "You shouldn't speak her name because she can *hear* you say it. She can hear every utterance of M-A-B."

"You...You're joking, right?" Saoirse's eyes grew wide as saucers, and she glanced around, suddenly paranoid. "That sounds like a god-tier power. Omniscience or something. She can't really do that, can she?"

"Saoirse," I said, "she could wipe all life off this planet if she wanted to. There is absolutely nothing beyond belief about her being able to hear her name when people use it aloud."

Saoirse was starting to look a lot paler than normal. "Fucking hell. I've been saying it all the time. I've been *swearing* at her all the time."

I snorted. "If it's any consolation, I can assure you she doesn't care about all the nasty things humans have to say about her. Or anything most fae have to say about her. Because you're not threatening to her in any way, shape, or form. You're, well, irrelevant."

"I'm an ant, you mean," Saoirse said flatly, "yelling at a boot hanging over my head."

"Yeah, that's about the gist of it."

"Well, that's a nice blow to my ego." She pinched the bridge of her nose. "But if she doesn't give a shit about what anyone says, why shouldn't I say her name now?"

"Because we're currently discussing a problem that would legitimately piss her off and bring her wrath down on Kinsale."

"Oh." Saoirse winced. "Got it."

"So, you want to move on from this riveting discussion about our beloved faerie queen and discuss the plan for stopping Mr. Harp Buyer from putting Kinsale in the line of fire?"

"I'm not sure it's a matter of desire so much as one of necessity, but okay."

We spent the next thirty minutes hashing out the first stage of our plot to foil a far worse plot. After which Saoirse plodded off with only an awkward wave for a goodbye so she could get ready to sneak into the auction tonight in my stead. Having my old partner put herself in the hot seat to get me out of a bind wasn't my favorite idea in the world, but at the same time, it was kind of nice to be working a "case" with Saoirse again. Even if we still couldn't bring ourselves to touch each other, or make eye contact for more than half a second at a time.

But what'll happen after this is over? I wondered. *We go back to the cold shoulder?*

Saoirse certainly seemed willing to speak to me in the same snarky manner we used to in the good old days, but how deep did that camaraderie run? How deep *could* it run after we'd parted on such awful terms? There was a massive gulf between us, a fracture that had cleaved the earth wide open on my last day as a cop, so vast and deep that I wasn't sure it could be crossed, much less mended. Even if we did somehow manage to stitch the damn thing closed, it wasn't as if the scars would disappear. The real ones or the emotional ones. No, the scars would always remain.

But did that mean it wasn't worth it to re-forge our friendship?

Ah hell. After seven years of practical isolation, I'm even worse at this relationship crap than I was before.

I pushed all my concerns to the back of my mind for the time being. If I spent the entire evening staring at wet tunnel walls while torturing myself over the sins of the past, I was going to lose my mind before Saoirse returned with the ledger. And being insane was not conducive to saving the city from a looming doom.

Plus, there were other topics that I needed to dwell on. Like plotting a continuous maze-like route through the tunnels that would keep the barghest baffled until Saoirse met with me at our next rendezvous point so we could head to the buyer's home.

I glanced left. Gurgling water and an endless tunnel that stretched into the abyss.

I glanced right. Gurgling water and an endless tunnel that stretched into the abyss.

It was going to be a long evening. I needed to start keeping snacks in my pocket.

CHAPTER ELEVEN

AT THE APPOINTED HOUR, I CHANGED MY ROUTE THROUGH the tunnels, found my designated exit point, climbed a ladder back to the surface, and punched open a grate that let me out in an alleyway between two abandoned buildings on Third Street. The night was damp and dark, no streetlights, electric or magic, to keep the shadows at bay. I stole through the darkness, eyes and ears alert, hunting for any signs of the barghest, and made my way down the empty street to the park bench across from a gutted Five Guys where Saoirse and I had eaten many a lunch way back when.

Saoirse wasn't at the bench when I arrived, and I didn't want to sit there alone and draw attention in case anyone walked by. So I hunkered down on the stoop of a nearby brick building that had once been a dentist's office, according to the curling, browned sign in the window. From there, I scoped out the entire neighborhood, made a list of all the places a paranormal hostile might lie in wait, and put a mental high-light on all the entry points to the street big enough for the barghest to navigate.

I wasn't exactly nervous—Saoirse knew what she was do-ing—but I kept counting down the minutes until the "split and run" deadline she'd given me. She'd explicitly told me not to wait if she didn't show on time, because she didn't want the barghest to track me down and use me like a chew toy. While I appreciated the concern, Saoirse showing up late, or not showing up at all, would mean something had gone horribly wrong. Because Saoirse Daly had never once, in all my years on the force, ever shown up late to the precinct, to a crime scene, or even to a colleague cookout in the boonies. She didn't *do* late. Unless she was dead or dying. Unless someone or something had—

A shadow fluttered in a nearby alley.

I snapped out of my reverie just in time to see Saoirse dart out into the street full speed. A messenger bag slung around her shoulder. A slinky black dress fit for a fancy function rid-ing up her thighs. Her bright red hair coming unwound from a complex coif. At some point, she'd lost her shoes, probably a pair of heels she couldn't run in, and she was treading rough pavement that was bound to have torn her skin. But if she was in pain, she didn't let it show. What she *did* let show was the terror.

The terror of being pursued by creatures of the night.

Out of the inky darkness of the alley emerged ten black-clad shapes wielding various pointy weapons. The humanoid creatures had washed-out gray skin, jet-black hair woven into elaborate braids, and eyes with black irises and silvery sclera that resembled liquid mercury, gleaming even in the perpetual gloom of a cloudy night. They snarled at Saoirse's hustling form, flashing shark-like teeth and releasing loud hisses that seemed to wrap around everything they touched and *squeeze*, a silken noose.

Svartálfar. Dark elves.

I was so shocked to see them on a random street in Kinsale, I just sat stupidly on the stoop, jaw hanging open. Dark elves rarely left Svartalfheim, their ancestral home realm, and even more rarely did they leave the Otherworld. Dark elves had what was practically an allergic reaction to direct sunlight—ironically, they fit the vampire mythos more than the actual vampires—so Earth, with its nice yellow dwarf hanging in the sky every day, was not a popular vacation destination for the meaner cousins of the common elf.

They also *hated* humans, more than most paranormal creatures. I'd encountered a dark elf exactly once before to-night, and he'd immediately tried to chop off my head with an axe for the mere insult of wearing a human glamour.

Yet here was a horde of them chasing a cop down a city street.

They can't be working for Bismarck, I realized with a sinking feeling. *They'd never make a deal with a human. That means they're working for Bismarck's partner. And that means Bismarck's partner isn't human.*

Just what I needed. A powerful nonhuman adversary.

I yanked myself back into the moment as Saoirse slipped on a slick patch of asphalt, nearly throwing herself into a nasty fall. She recovered but lost her lead on the dark elves, who hissed in anticipation and raised their weapons as they closed in on the cop still struggling to regain her footing. Saoirse knew she'd lost the chase, so she didn't try to keep running. Instead, she stuffed her hand into the messenger bag and tugged out a handgun, flipping the safety off with a swift flick of her thumb. Then she took a defensive stance and let the elf bastards have it.

The first bullet nailed the closest dark elf in the face, and he went back spewing blood from the socket where his eye had been. The second bullet caught another elf in the neck, and he spun around in a dancer-like manner, a fountain of blood spurting from a severed vessel. The third elf in the lineup wised up and raised a quick shield, but Saoirse's third bullet plowed through it like glass and plunged into the elf's chest with so much force he was actually flung backward. He collided with two of his friends, who were bowled over onto their asses.

The whole time this onslaught was occurring, Saoirse's gun was faintly glowing green.

Charmed. By a fairly powerful practitioner too, judging by the strength of the shots.

(I had a funny feeling that wasn't a standard-issue PD weapon.)

But it wasn't going to be enough. The elves had been holding back when they thought Saoirse wasn't a threat. They'd been treating her like helpless prey, thinking if they followed her long enough she'd eventually run out of stamina and become easy pickings, a fragile thing they could torture to their hearts' content. The joke was on them, and they'd now realized it. The sight of their fallen comrades spurred their fury, and they amped up their magic energy. Dark, mist-like auras coalesced around their bodies. A tangible taste of magic, thick and pungent, hung in the air.

Saoirse's fourth bullet ricocheted off the next elf's shield and ate into the pavement.

That was my cue.

I leaped from the stoop, held up my hand, and released all the energy I'd been gathering in my palm. It blasted outward, shrieking like a brutal winter gale, and struck the three elves at the head of the charging group with the force of a speeding train. One of them was flung straight through a window and crashed into a pile of furniture in a defunct living room. One of them slammed into the brick façade of the same town-house, breaking half his bones. And the third, who was caught at an awkward angle at the edge of the magic blast, rammed headfirst into an old metal USPS mailbox. His skull didn't survive the impact.

The four remaining dark elves skidded to a stop and whipped their heads toward me.

"Unseelie half-blood," one of them said in a raspy voice. "You've made a grave mistake."

"I've made a lot of grave mistakes, pal." I subtly tapped the fingers of my left hand against my thigh in a pattern I hoped Saoirse remembered. *Fall back on my word.* "Have yet to end up in a hole I can't dig myself out of."

He hissed, flashing those creepy teeth. "There always comes a day."

A curved ice dagger formed in my outstretched hand, and I pointed the tip at the elf's face. "You think that day is today? Prove it, bucko."

At the word "bucko," Saoirse turned on her toes and sprinted down the street. The dark elf who'd spoken to me immediately launched into another pursuit. A dark cloud of magic energy built up around one hand, his arm poised to throw a deadly spell at my old partner's retreating form. But before he made it three steps, I slung the dagger at him. It whizzed by his face, cutting through his now fully powered shield in a way Saoirse's charmed bullets couldn't dream of, and took off the end of his nose.

He staggered to a stop as blood ran over his lips and chin, dripped onto the asphalt at his feet. He prodded the wound, perplexed, then followed the trajectory of the dagger—and found it lodged inside the skull of the elf who'd collided with the brick façade. The other three elves, who'd made to follow their de facto leader after Saoirse, now stood stock-still, glancing between the dead elf with the ice blade sticking out of his head, and the half-fae who'd dared to throw it. Until de facto leader elf made a slow, counterclockwise turn toward me and said, "Kill him."

In the corner of my eye, I caught Saoirse darting into an alley, safe from any direct lines of fire. I wanted to tell her to keep on running, because this was about to get nasty, but there was no point. Saoirse wouldn't leave me in the middle of a fight. Even if she was hurt. Even if she was dying. And I wouldn't leave her either.

Except for that one time, said a derisive mental voice, *you left her for seven years.*

I shook off the guilty thought as the four dark elves dashed toward me, and summoned another surge of power. My magic, having tasted the blood of an enemy paranormal, was all too happy to comply. It practically giggled as it flooded my entire body, urging me to fight, kill, destroy, *annihilate*. It rose from the surface of my skin like mist rising from the earth in the wake of a damaging storm. When I exhaled a string of words, sharp and cold, ice crystals crackled in the air around me and formed a field of spinning blades even sharper than the one I'd used before.

I snatched a blade from the space beside me, locked eyes with the elf missing the tip of his nose, and attacked. Surging forward, I mentally pushed the blades around me into a whirling tempest. They arced through the air, coming at the elves from all directions. Two of the elves broke off from the oncoming group as they struggled to dodge and parry so many projectiles at once, but the leader and one other, a female elf, expertly avoided the blades and countered with spells of their own.

The woman vanished in a puff of black smoke, only to reappear behind me, her short sword already swinging toward my neck. I dodged the blow by a hair and swung my ice dagger at her abdomen, only for the blade to shatter before it made contact. It was struck by rigid black strings crackling with electricity, which stretched from the *fingernails* of the lead elf. The strings suddenly cut a hard left and shot toward my chest, and I had to drop to my knees to avoid getting skewered. Which put me directly in the downward arc of the woman's next swing.

Even with my unglamoured speed, I couldn't move in time.

So I buffered my palms with absorbent blocks of energy and *caught* the sword. The force of the blow nearly sent me sprawling. But I braced myself against the asphalt, then jerked to the right, under the vibrating black strings still hanging in the air, and heaved myself into a standing position, dragging the blade of the sword along with me. The instant the blade made contact with the strings, I let it go—the elf woman wasn't so lucky. She realized what was happening a fraction of a second too late. Just as a violent bolt of electricity leaped from the strings, down the length of the sword blade, and into her hands.

Thunder roared. The sword exploded in a blinding flash, and the woman shot across the street and slammed into the stoop I'd been sitting on earlier. The concrete cracked underneath her back, and her head smacked the railing with a clang loud enough to wake the dead. Pieces of her shattered sword, edges blackened from the sheer power of the electricity spell, clattered onto the asphalt and sidewalk, smoking.

Ha! Not bad for an unpracticed—

A second sword swung into view. I flung myself to the side, but the tip of the blade sliced through my left ear, nearly splitting it in half. Pain lanced across my head, but it wasn't iron pain—their weapons were made of an Otherworld metal. I was able to clamp the pain down by refocusing my heightened senses elsewhere. Then I recovered my stance by pushing off the asphalt with one hand, and hopped back into the fray with my bloodthirsty magic prepped for round two. Just as the lead elf followed through on his swing, did a total three-sixty, and came around for another blow.

I drove my fist at his chest in an attempt to pull the same ice spike move I'd used on the half-troll, while I held up my other arm, forming a small but dense shield with a single whispered word to block the oncoming sword. But when my knuckles were two inches from his soiled shirt, a flying dagger snuck in between my hand and his chest. The instant the fabric of my glove touched it, a wall of pure force crashed into my body and flung me fifteen feet down the street.

I landed in a painful roll but forced myself back up as the lead elf and one of the others—who'd smashed all the ice blades I sent spinning his way—ran at me full speed, each wielding a weapon and a waiting spell.

The new entrant into this fight pulled the same teleportation trick as his female colleague, appearing in the space behind me, a few feet off the ground. I was ready for him. Spitting out a guttural string of words, I summoned a powerful vortex of air, dragging him out of his trajectory and around my body in a wide arc.

The man was thrown in front of me at the same moment the lead elf lunged forward so he could perform a quick, devastating hit with his sword while simultaneously shooting another round of those creepy black strings from his free hand. The leader couldn't abort the maneuver in time. So the sword ran the other elf through, and the black strings struck the man's face, impaling his brain and electrocuting him to death.

The lead elf then lost his footing in shock and barreled into his dead colleague. I jumped high enough to avoid the resulting tangle of body parts, landed in a crouch, and…nearly fainted. Not from exhaustion, but from the sheer overwhelming force of my own magic's visceral ferocity slamming into the barrier that was my fourth glamour. My vision faded to pinpoints. My hearing was muted. My skin lost its sensitivity, and I couldn't even feel the weight of my clothes. My taste and smell went haywire, nothing but the clean scent of a deep winter tingling in my throat.

I'd pushed myself too hard. I'd used too many combat spells, hurt or killed too many people, and now my magic was aching to find its real home, its real form, to reach its true potential. It could feel its own unbounded self lurking somewhere behind my deeper glamours, a faint, unyielding flicker of frosty light in the distance that could grow into a blizzard of epic proportions, wreak untold destruction, destroy my enemies with a single breath, bring the entire city to heel beneath its might. If only I would set it free, unleash its awful strength unto this petty, weak human world full of fragile, disgusting little things—

A gunshot yanked me from the brink.

The world shifted back into focus.

I spun around to see the other elf who'd been busy smashing my spinning ice blades collapse in a pool of his own blood and brain matter. He'd been about two steps from cutting me clean in half with his sword. At the end of the alley down the street, Saoirse lowered her gun and mouthed, *Are you all right?*

Was I? I didn't know. I'd almost let my damn faerie magic drive me to the point of stripping the rest of my glamours. The last time I'd let that urge get the better of me, I'd been *twelve*.

I couldn't be this reckless. I couldn't risk waking that beast. Not to beat these dark elves. Not to beat the barghest. I'd legitimately forgotten until this very moment just how brutal and merciless and callous the nature of my true self really was. I'd spent so many years with my base glamours perfectly intact, not a scratch, my magic use minimal and safe, that I'd lost sight of the monstrous creature that lurked beneath my skin.

That was close. Way too close.

I forced myself to nod at Saoirse, then turned around to confront the lead elf, who was busy extricating himself from the corpse of his fallen colleague. Instead of using any more of my magic, I grabbed the hilt of his sword and tugged it from the dead elf with a wet squelch. I held the bloodstained tip an inch from the leader's bloody nose, threatening to chop off the rest of it with a swift flick of my wrist. He stopped trying to rise and remained on his knees, his head tipped up toward me, pointy teeth on show in a wide sneer. "You're a trifling bastard, half-blood."

"Nice to know I haven't lost my touch." I jerked the blade a hairsbreadth closer to his skin. He flinched. I smiled. "So, you want to give up the ghost and tell me who the hell you're working for? Because I'm getting kind of hungry, and I turn into a real sourpuss when I miss dinner."

The elf's bloody sneer slowly morphed into a smirk. "We operate on contracts much the same as the fae," he said, lapping a streak of blood off his lip. "A fact of which I'm sure you are aware. I cannot speak the name of my employer out loud, or write it down, by an explicit clause in the contract under which I'm currently operating. Very unfortunate for you, to have expended so much energy, only to gain no real intelligence in the end."

"I've gained plenty of 'intelligence' about your so-called employer," I retorted. "Namely, that he—"

"Vince!" Saoirse cried out.

About one-quarter of a second before an iron poker side-swiped my left arm.

CHAPTER TWELVE

THE POINT OF THE POKER TORE THROUGH THE FABRIC OF MY coat and shirt, exposing my skin to the length of the rod as it rocketed past, launched in a powerful javelin toss by the female elf who'd been thrown through the townhouse window a few minutes prior. The sharp point didn't pierce me, but it didn't have to. The mere brush of the metal against my arm dissolved layers of skin, as if I'd been splattered with a strong acid. Pain like white-hot fire exploded through my entire arm, left shoulder, neck, and head.

I dropped the sword, collapsed to my knees, and screamed as I uselessly grasped at the sizzling wound spreading across my arm, blood weeping out, blisters and red sores disfiguring flesh the poker hadn't even touched. At the rim of the field of inflamed skin, hives started to break out in all directions, crawling up my neck and across my back and down the length of my arm, itching worse than any human allergic reaction ever could, urging me to flay myself raw. It was as if I'd been stung by the most potently venomous creature on the planet.

And my magic couldn't *stand it*. Iron was anathema to the very nature of the fae.

The power inside me went wild, devolving into a beast from the dawn of creation, raving and spitting and screeching, clawing through my brain and beating at my skull so hard I swore my head would explode. I desperately tried to maintain control, but the pain of the iron burn was so overwhelming, I couldn't think straight, and my magic was so riled up, between the injury and the combat spells I'd been overusing, that I started to lose my grip on it. The magic writhed and wrestled with me, demanding I set it free, pounding the gates of my glamours. And as the lead elf bent down and grabbed his sword, preparing to take off my head with a swift blow, my infuriated magic finally got the better of me.

For half a second, I lost control.

That was enough.

My fourth glamour cracked like an egg, and half the mask that concealed my face, my real face, fell away. I whipped my head up and snarled at the lead elf, driven into a rage by my frenzied magic as a tsunami of power rose from within me and threatened to crash out into the world beyond my body, drowning and destroying everything in its path. A hundred million possible spells at my fingertips, ready and aching to annihilate my enemies, the ancient power of the fae rearing its head from a place I'd been desperately hoping to keep it bottled up forever. Power that could…Power that wanted… Power…

The lead elf was staring at me in abject horror. His sword, raised at a sharp angle, didn't budge from its position. The smug satisfaction that had been budding inside him at the sight of me on my knees, vulnerable, had crumbled to dust and left a deep-seated fear in its wake. Now, all he could do was focus on the jagged hole left by my partially broken glamour. On the face beneath the cracked mask. On my real eye. On the marks around that eye. On the lethal implications of those two simple features.

"You…" he stammered. "You're no lesser fae. You're a—"

His sentence was choked off by the blade I rammed through his chest. While his attention had been so helpfully glued to my exposed face, I'd reached back with my right hand and snatched the sword held in the limp fingers of the elf Saoirse shot dead a moment ago. Then I simply slid the sword up through his abdomen, under his ribs, and into his heart.

Yet despite the mortal wound draining the life from his body, the dark elf still kept ogling my face, lips moving soundlessly in what was either an expression of useless apology or a hopeless prayer to an Otherworld god. Right up until the second his consciousness flickered out for good and he collapsed backward onto the corpse of the colleague he'd accidentally skewered.

More gunshots sounded off behind me, and I turned—to the right—and caught sight of Saoirse firing at the last elf standing, the woman who'd thrown the poker. The woman's shield was holding, bullets pinging off, but she was badly injured from being slung into the townhouse by my earlier spell. She didn't have enough strength to counter the bullets and attack me at the same time. So I grabbed the sword from the hand of her dead leader, took aim, and threw it at her the same way she'd thrown the poker at me.

It pierced her back and emerged from her chest, cleaving her heart in two. She fell.

Silence veiled the street.

Saoirse searched for any more hostiles in the area before she came running over. I slapped my left hand over the exposed side of my face, ignoring the sharp pain in my upper arm, so Saoirse wouldn't see what the lead elf had. She slid to a stop beside me and dropped to one knee, gaze roving over my body, on the hunt for serious injuries. "Are you okay?" she said. "I thought you were going to die like six times. Jesus. Don't scare me like that."

"Scare you?" I let out a weak laugh. "You're the one who came running into the neighborhood with a horde of dark elves on your ass."

"Is that what they are?" She looked at the dead elves scattered around the block. "I had no clue. They showed up out of nowhere about two blocks from the auction house and gave chase." She leaned closer to my arm to examine the aggravated wound. "That looks nasty. Is it a poison?"

"Iron."

Her lips parted in a quiet gasp. "What did she throw?"

"A poker. I assume from someone's fireplace." I nodded toward the townhouse with the broken living room window. "It's not a big deal. It just grazed my arm. It'll heal."

"It looks so painful though."

"It *is* painful, and extremely itchy. Not unlike an allergic reaction. Iron and faeries don't mix—in the worst of ways."

She sighed. "I'm so sorry I let them get the drop on me. Now you're hurt in my place."

"Bullshit." I braced myself against the asphalt with my good hand and pushed myself to my feet on wobbly legs,

Saoirse's helping hands hovering nearby in case I stumbled. "I'm the one who dragged you into this ridiculous game. I only have myself to blame for letting 'Tom' trick me into searching for the harp."

"But if you hadn't gone after the harp, then the buyer would've been able to cast this awful spell unimpeded, right?" She cocked an eyebrow. "So it's a damn good thing Tom did lure you into this mess, at least for the well-being of Kinsale." She gestured to my torn, disheveled clothing and myriad injuries. "Obviously, not for *your* well-being."

"What about you? You hurt?"

"Nothing serious. A few cuts and bruises. I'll live." Her hands drifted toward my face. "I see your ear is hanging on by a thread, but did you take a blow to your eye too? I can check and see how bad it—"

"It's fine." I pushed magic into the charm on my necklace that housed my fourth glamour and mentally shouted the words to patch the crack around my face. When I was finished, the resulting mask wasn't flawless—most paranormals could see through it if they concentrated—but it was enough to fool a human with no magic-powered sight. So I dropped my hand, showing my fake face to Saoirse. "See? Just took a glancing blow with a hilt. Got a little rattled."

She pursed her lips, unconvinced, but she let the matter drop for now. Patting her messenger bag, she said, "I got the ledger. I was planning to just find the entry for the harp buyer and copy the name and address, but one of the guards walked in while I was perusing. So I had to cut and run. Though I don't really guess subtlety matters much at this point, since Bismarck already knows you're on the case."

I shook my head. "We're past the point of being sneaky."

I gestured to the bloody battle scene around us. "These elves are the buyer's mooks, not Bismarck's. He knows we're onto him, and he knows we're coming. Might as well plow ahead."

"So, where to now?" She wrapped her bare arms around her torso, suppressing a shiver. The night was cold and getting colder, and Saoirse was wearing nothing but a cocktail dress.

"You got a change of clothes?"

"In the bag. But I'd prefer not changing in the middle of a street. Or in a flood tunnel."

"Good point." I looked both ways down the street. "A lot of the buildings around here are empty. Could just jimmy the lock on one and change inside real quick."

"Ah, breaking and entering," she mused, "such exemplary behavior for a cop."

"If it makes you feel any better, most of the people who owned these buildings are dead."

She gave me a flat stare. "Thanks, Vince, for yet another dose of cynical—"

A loud growl rumbled down the street, echoed into the alleys, shook the ground beneath my feet. I spun on my heels, nearly stumbling from the combined strain of my injuries and the mental exhaustion of fighting a tug-o-war with my own nonhuman magic. Standing a block away, having somehow snuck up on us while we were talking, was the barghest. I was baffled as to how it had managed to enter the neighborhood without setting off any of my sensory alarms. I should've heard it, seen it, *felt* it, since it was following my scent and was thus tangible to me. Unless someone else had veiled...

In the space around the barghest, half a dozen dark elves stripped off veils like they were tugging off cloaks. The skin on the back of my neck prickled, and I peered over my shoulder, to find *another* six elves half a block behind Saoirse and me.

I've been played, I realized. *Yet again.*

They'd surrounded us while we were busy taking out the last few members of the vanguard. More than that, the whole point of the first ten chasing Saoirse was so I'd reveal myself, intervene to help her, and then get delayed in a fight with a numbers disadvantage that would wear me out. Tired and injured, I would be easy pickings for a dozen more elves plus a barghest. And Saoirse would be too, because she was only human and didn't have infinite bullets.

Together, the twelve dark elves and the big black dog were to be our execution squad.

"Well, shit," Saoirse muttered. "Now what?"

A good question. One I didn't have a simple answer for.

"Tell me, do you see the barghest?" I whispered.

"I assume that's the giant black dog-looking thing?"

I made a disapproving click of my tongue. "If you can see it, it has your scent too, and that means it plans to kill you."

"Lovely." She inched closer to me. "So, is this going to be a 'go out with guns blazing' situation, or are you going to pull a sweet magic trick out of your ass and save us?"

"Out of my ass? What do you take me for, an amateur?"

"Actually, I did take you for an amateur"—she pulled a new magazine out of her bag and swapped it for the empty one in her gun—"until I watched you take down those elves just now. I had no idea you could use magic that powerful. And I'm substantially more afraid than I was before."

My stomach tightened. "Afraid of me?"

Her eyes met mine, wide with surprise. "What? No. I'm *impressed* with you. It's our enemies I'm afraid of. When you said you had to go all out to beat the bar…the dog thing, I honestly had no frame of reference for how much power you were talking about. Assuming that what you just displayed fighting these elves wasn't 'all out'—which I take to be true since you don't look any more fae than you did before—then that means the dog monster is far, far stronger than I was imagining. Which, as a magicless human armed with only a weak charmed weapon, is a terrifying idea."

"Oh." Some of the ice weighing down my stomach began to melt. "I'm impressive, huh?"

"We can discuss the finer details of your badassery later, Vince. You know, if we're not dead."

"We can discuss them even if we are dead, you know? Just in a less physical state."

She frowned. "Can we focus on the death squad and how to escape them? Please?"

"Actually, that's what I'm doing." And I was. Currently cycling through every possible escape strategy in the known universe. But I was coming up dry. I was starting to think I might need to look at escape routes in *other* universes. "Adding a dash of humor to situations where I'm on the verge of death makes it a tad easier for me to think over the terrified internal screaming."

"I see," she said, tightening her grip on the gun as the elves in front of us began to move. "Should I start telling jokes?"

"You got booed off a stand-up stage once, so I'm going to say no." I glanced behind us. The rearguard was closing in as well, one slow, even step at a time. They were all moving in to form a tight circle we couldn't breach, at which point they would attack simultaneously with a host of sharp swords and pointy daggers and nasty spells. The barghest, on the other hand, was staying put. If Saoirse and I somehow managed to evade the elves, the creature would intervene and rip us to shreds. Considering it was intelligent, I doubted it would allow me to pull the flood tunnel trick a second time.

We were well and truly screwed if we stayed here a minute longer.

"Fucking hell," I said. "We really have no choice. I'm going to have to call in my marker."

"Marker?" Saoirse paused with her gun halfway up. "With who?"

"Hard to explain. Better see for yourself." I flexed my hand a couple of times, vacillating over whether to reach out and grab her. We hadn't breached each other's personal space even once since our initial encounter at Mo's shop this morning, a seven-year wedge of bad blood and haunting memories stuck in between us.

But I knew it was foolish to dwell on the past, especially during a situation whose outcome would decide the future. Saoirse wasn't to blame for what happened to me, and I had no reason to keep my distance from her other than to keep my distance from her workplace and her coworkers. An issue that was not hard to manage, and never had been. I'd just spent the time I should've been repairing the bridge between us wrapped in a bitter blanket and cursing my circumstances.

If my dad had been alive, he would've verbally beaten me for wallowing in self-pity.

Get your act together, Whelan. It's time to act like a mature adult.

I took a deep breath, and let it out.

Then I grabbed Saoirse's wrist and yanked her toward me, wrapping my other arm around her waist to pull her flush against my chest. Her cheek brushed mine, the one with the patchwork glamour, and her warmth bled through the faulty spell, tingling against my wintery skin. She let out a hushed gasp at the contact, and made to ask me what the heck I was doing, but I cut her off and said, "Hold on to me, tightly, and do not, under any circumstances, let go until I tell you to. Understand?"

She went rigid, hesitating, for only a second. Before she hugged me in a way that spoke of more than necessity (though I didn't have time to dwell on *that* right now). "Whatever you're about to do better be damn impressive. Because we have one shot at getting out of this trap before we end up shish kebabs."

The elves were moving in quicker now, alerted by our movements.

"It's not what I'm about to do you have to worry about. It's what happens afterward."

"What do you—?"

I stomped one foot, channeling all the energy I could muster into the ground beneath me. Frost shot out in all directions, curling and crackling across the asphalt, forming lines and shapes, symbols and words, until all the components joined together, closing to create the most fundamental method of magic casting in existence. A circle. Whose purpose any novice could read with a few language references, and which the elves immediately recognized. The barghest figured it out too, and at the same moment, all of our adversaries bounded forward, desperate to reach us before I spoke the invocation.

Funny thing was, I didn't need to use an invocation.

All I had to do was think: *Take me home.*

A wall of wind and snow shot up from the edge of the

circle, blocking every sword and knife as the elves attempted
to skewer us. The ground began to shift beneath our feet, until it became like quicksand, slowly drawing us down, down,
down. Saoirse stiffened in fear, her heart pounding against her
ribs. I embraced her securely, reassuring, as the ground ceased
to exist altogether, as our heads slipped beneath the pavement,
out of the meager light of a Kinsale night and into the total
darkness of the space between worlds.

We fell through infinite blackness for what seemed an
eternity. Until, out of nowhere, we bumped into something
hard. Something that rebuffed us the way a hammer hits a
nail, driving us back so fast we sprang off into the deepness as
if shot from a cannon. We hurtled through the void, clinging
to each other, spinning head over feet, feet over head, until
finally our soles came into contact with a barrier whose touch
was not unlike the soft caress of silk. It stopped our movement, instantly, yet without inertia crushing us to pieces, no
laws of physics binding us, reality but a dream. And for a moment in a place beyond time and space, we stood untethered
from the universe.

Then the silken floor upon which we stood...*spun*. The
void fled from existence, and a new reality bled in.

I blinked the vestiges of darkness away and found myself
standing on an ocean.

CHAPTER THIRTEEN

THE WORLD WAS BRIGHT, BUT THE SKY WASN'T BLUE. INSTEAD, we stood beneath a black dome of space populated by the scattered realms of the Otherworld. Some realms were distant lights, like stars, while others were close, the colorful features of places strange and foreign to Earth cast across the horizon. There were realms that looked to be planets, with vast rings of glass and stone arced around them. There were realms that looked to be flat planes, oceans cascading off their edges and billowing out into cosmic clouds. There were realms that looked to be things I couldn't even describe, because the words to describe such things didn't exist in any language I knew.

Saoirse disentangled herself from me and staggered back, thrown off kilter by the strange sights around her. She stared first at her bare, scraped feet, standing atop a gently rocking ocean, unable to penetrate its surface. Confused, she lifted one foot, a drop of blood rolling off a cut on her toe and splattering *on*to the water. The drop undulated with the movement of the waves, but it didn't sink into the water and disperse. It was like the ocean was a tilting floor beneath our feet. And really, that wasn't far off from the truth.

Saoirse's wide brown eyes drifted up to the sky then, and her mouth dropped open in awe. She spun around, seeking anything recognizable, but north and south and east and west, there was nothing but water as far as any eye could see. Down there was nothing but ocean, crystal clear near its surface and black near its base, if there *was* a base. Up there was nothing but space and the realms that occupied it, too far away for us to touch.

Eventually, Saoirse found her wits and said, "Vince, where are we?"

"It's got a lot of names. The Endless Sea. The Sea Between Worlds. The Sea of Lost Souls." I swiped my foot along the surface of the water. If I pushed hard enough, I could make it ripple, but I couldn't punch through it. "You can call it whatever you want."

"But *what* is it? And why are we standing on it instead of swimming in it?"

"It's a body of water that exists between all the realms of the Otherworld." I pointed at the heavily populated sky above. "See those? The ocean exists between all those realms."

"Huh?" She squinted as she catalogued all the celestial bodies floating above us. "But those are planets of some kind, in space. How can the ocean exist between them? I don't understand."

"No one understands." I chuckled. "It just *is*."

She clenched her eyes shut and smacked her cheeks a couple times, something she always did whenever she was stressed and needed to focus. Eyes fluttering open again, she said, "I'm guessing everything in the Otherworld makes as much sense as that explanation?"

"Par for the course." I gestured to the water beneath us. "And as for why we're standing on the water, it's because we're not 'compatible' with it. The Endless Sea is not a place inhabited by the living. The spirits of the ocean live here, along with the souls of the dead who've lost their way on their journey into the afterlife."

Saoirse squinted as she scoured the depths of the water. She pointed her finger at something. "Is that an ocean spirit or a dead person?"

I followed her finger to a bioluminescent blue streak flittering through the water well over a hundred feet below the surface. "Ah, that's a fuath. They're the guardians of the sea—and angry little bastards."

Saoirse pursed her lips. "Will they hurt us?"

"Nah. Sometimes, they venture into other bodies of water, in the Otherworld and on Earth, at which point they're liable to attack people. But since living people can't enter the Endless Sea, and the shades of the dead are intangible to the fuathan, they don't usually get aggressive here."

"Well, at least there's some kind of paranormal not after our heads." She immediately grimaced. "Sorry. I know you're a paranormal too. I just…" She let out a deep sigh. "Apparently, I've gotten really bad at talking to you."

"Seven years will do that." I took a better look at my injured arm. The wound wasn't deep, but it was extremely tender, and every twitch of my muscles sent another wave of fiery pain up my neck. It wasn't unmanageable though. I could grin and bear it for a while. And I had a salve at home crafted specifically for iron wounds. It wouldn't accelerate the healing—nothing could, since iron burned faeries all the way down to the soul—but it would take most of the pain away so I wouldn't have to dwell on it for the weeks it took to mend.

Saoirse shuffled closer to me, her footing unsteady, and eyed the wound, frowning. "That won't scar, will it?"

I bit the inside of my cheek. "Hate to break it to you, but all iron wounds scar."

"All?" She blinked owlishly at me, like she didn't fully understand, before the implication smacked her in the face. "You mean, the injuries from the chain that they…"

I nodded.

She slapped a hand over her mouth. "Oh, Vince. I'm so…" Her gaze fell to my chest, boring through my shirt fabric, seeking out any hint of the pale, patterned marks permanently branded on my skin. "I'm so sorry," she finished weakly.

"You didn't do it. You have nothing to be sorry about."

She hung her head. "You're wrong. I was there. I could've stopped them."

I opened my mouth to contradict her, but struggled to push out the words. I'd let my anger and bitterness and depression over the attack simmer for so many years that it'd painted anyone and everyone who'd even been in the vicinity of the precinct during the time in a negative light. I'd justified my loathing of all those people, Saoirse included, by telling myself exactly what she had just said: that they could've done something to help me. Even though I'd known all along that excuse for such aching hatred was bunk. Even though I knew there was no one to blame but the bigots who'd actually done the deed.

The breakdown of all my relationships at the precinct—
relationships with good people, like Saoirse—was not the fault
of the seven men who'd wrapped me in an iron chain and
beaten me to a pulp the day I slipped up and revealed my paranormal heritage to one of them by accident. The breakdown
was my fault. I'd let the trauma get the better of me. I'd used it
as a free ride to spit nasty things at my own partner, call her so
many derogatory names that ought to have earned me a one-
way ticket to hell. I'd used it to smear all my best memories
of my time as a cop with an ugly, oily poison. And then I'd
used those soiled memories as fuel for my coldly burning fury.

It was so hypocritical of me, to act like all humans—in
particular, all cops—were as bad as those men. Considering
how many humans had treated paranormals the same way,
as if we were all evil creatures aligned with the devil. Yet I'd
ridden that hypocrisy for so long, seven goddamn years, because at the end of the day, I was a coward who didn't want
to confront the pain of the past and sort out the jagged pieces
of myself to build a better future. Because I was too afraid of
getting cut all over again.

Saoirse had endlessly suffered in her own emotional prison
as a result of my actions, blaming herself for my misfortune
this whole time. And she didn't deserve it. Not one bit.

*It's far past time you rectify this, you absolute bastard. You
owed her an apology years ago.*

Fingers shaking, I stripped off my right glove, reached
out, and took Saoirse's hand. "No. You couldn't have stopped
them. You couldn't have done anything. If you'd tried, they'd
have hurt you too, for being a sympathizer."

She squeezed my hand, her own quaking badly. "I had a
gun. I could've done something."

"Not without destroying your entire life. You'd have been marked. You'd have lost your job. You'd have lost your home. You'd have been forced to run. You would've had to go underground with me, and the underground was not a good place for a human during the purge. You'd have been miserable and constantly in danger." I rubbed my thumb across her knuckles. "I wouldn't have wanted that for you, living such a perilous existence for months on end. It's better that you didn't intervene until the attack was over. That decision kept you safe."

I smiled, weary. "Plus, it saved my life."

Saoirse's hand tightened around mine, and she said, breathless, "What do you mean?"

"After they were done kicking the shit out of me, they left me in that alley with the chain wrapped around my torso. Iron eats through faerie skin like acid, Saoirse. If you hadn't come along afterward and removed the chain, then the iron would've killed me."

"Oh my god."

"So, you see, if you'd gotten hurt or locked up trying to stop those men, I wouldn't even be here talking to you right now. I'd be in a shallow grave somewhere. Or ash in the air, like most of the purge victims."

Saoirse's eyes filled with tears, but they didn't fall. She surged forward and embraced me, burying her face in my shoulder, her breaths shuddering as she said, "I spent so long thinking you hated me."

"I pretended to," I said, guilt grating across my voice, "but in reality, I was just too spineless to approach humans the way I had before, and I channeled that fear into anger." I wrapped my arms around her, gently. "That crap I said to you after you unwrapped the chain and helped me out of the alley, when I threw your kindness back in your face…you should've hated *me* for that. Not the other way around. I'm sorry, Saoirse. I'm the one who threw our friendship away."

Saoirse brought her face directly in line with mine, then slowly tipped forward until our foreheads touched. "I'm starting to think pretty much everyone acted like a fool during this purge-war-collapse mess. And I'm inclined to forgive most people for running around like chickens with their heads cut off. So how about we agree to stop being a couple of needlessly guilty morons, and pick up where we left off? And if we can't pick it up, if that bridge is simply too damaged to repair, then how about we start over and build a new one?"

The tension that had been clutching my heart since Saoirse first walked into view at Mo's finally began to loosen. "I'll do whatever you think is best. You're the tactician after all. I'm the nimrod who jumps fences into yards with large guard dogs and nearly gets eaten alive."

Saoirse smiled, a real smile. "I told you to go another half block over."

"I thought I knew better back then." I smiled too. "I've learned from that mistake. And others."

We released each other, and she stepped back. "Good to hear. Why don't you show me what you've learned?" She gestured to the expanse of churning water that stretched on to every horizon. "What's the game plan? I assume you didn't bring us here for no reason."

"You think right. I did it to throw off the svartálfar and the barghest. You remember when we were traveling, that part where it felt like we bumped into something and bounced off?"

She thought for a moment, lips skewed to the side. "Vaguely."

"That was us getting repelled by the protective shield around the Unseelie Court's capital city. I intentionally directed my Otherworld portal to a location in the city so that the shield would rebuff us. Because when your portal fails to open at your designated exit point, you automatically get sent to a random location in the Endless Sea. And random means…"

"Your enemies can't follow you?" she finished.

"Exactly. They've lost us. And have no way to find us as long as we're here. Tracking spells don't work in the Endless Sea due to its wonky geography."

"Sweet." She arched an eyebrow. "But we do have to leave at some point."

"I am aware, thank you."

She snorted. "What's our next move then?"

"I call in a favor with someone who can drop us off in the right place for a slip portal."

"A what now?"

"A slip portal." I waved my hand in the air in a way that did not clarify anything. "There are multiple types of portals for crossing the veil between Earth and an Otherworld realm. Two of them are fairly standard: a directed portal and a slip portal. Directed portals require more power, but they let you come out anywhere—unshielded—that you want. A slip portal requires less power, but only lets you move between areas in the two realms that correspond to each other geographically. The upside of a slip portal, besides that it requires less magic expenditure, is that it's also practically unnoticeable. Direct portals are 'loud,' magically speaking."

"I see. So by using a slip portal to get back to Earth, those creepy elf people…"

"Svartálfar," I supplied.

"…and the dog monster won't immediately notice our return."

"Which is especially important"—I pointed to Saoirse's messenger bag—"considering I want to bring us out at the harp buyer's address."

"Ah. A sneak attack." She opened the bag, dug around for a second, and pulled out a leather-bound green notebook I assumed was the ledger. "Sounds like a plan. My only concern is that the address listed here isn't going to be an active base."

"I think it will be."

"Why?"

"Arrogance. This guy sent a horde of dark elves after us, plus a barghest, and I bet he's got plenty more where that came from. With that many resources at his disposal, he's bound to be overconfident." I flicked the top of the ledger. "And even if that address isn't our perp's main base of operations, I bet you a hundred chits we'll find something there that leads us to the real deal. This guy's planning to cast a spell that'll make the faerie *queens* angry. He's only worried about our interference insomuch as it risks alerting the fae to his plans too early. He doesn't actually think we can stop him. And that hubris—"

"—will lead him to make a critical mistake somewhere along the line." Saoirse nodded. "I see you've kept my lessons fresh."

"I would never let them fade."

"All right." She flipped through the ledger until she found a dog-eared page, then ran her finger down lines scrawled in ink until she found one near the bottom. She turned the ledger around and tapped on the entry. "The name is listed as 'Adam Smith,' which is obviously fake. But the address is legit. There's also a note underneath that confirms the harp was delivered to the house after the auction. I don't think they would've bothered to jot that down if they'd actually sent it elsewhere, considering they didn't suspect anyone was onto them the night of the auction. What do you think?"

The address was for a nondescript middle-class residential area on the edge of Kinsale, which actually made me more confident our perp would be there. It was a perfect place to hide a secret operation to cast a powerful spell away from the watching eyes of the local faerie bureaucrats and their dullahan enforcers. Who would suspect there was any funny business going down in a cul-de-sac full of family homes with patios and pools? And if somebody caught a whiff of something not quite right in the land of big lawns and barbecues, the neighborhood was far enough from downtown that most of what passed for Kinsale's government still wouldn't be concerned enough to check it out.

The fae were lazy as hell when it came to governing Earth.

That was going to come back to bite them in the ass sooner or later. Maybe tonight, if Saoirse and I failed to stop the harp buyer.

"Looks promising," I said to Saoirse. "There's no large population out that way. Less risk for collateral damage. And far enough out from City Hall that hopefully our unelected mayor and his friends won't notice anything amiss until we have a handle on the situation. If possible, I'd like to keep them from noticing at all."

Saoirse huffed. "Tell me about it. They almost never

interfere in police business, but when they do, it's a cluster-fuck every time."

"Sounds about right for the faerie elite. They love being obstructive manipulators."

"No offense to one half of your bloodline, but faeries suck in some pretty significant ways."

"Oh, no offense taken. You're a hundred percent correct."

She snapped the ledger shut and tucked it away in her bag again. "All right. I think we've dallied enough. What's next on the agenda? You said something about calling in a favor?"

"Yep. Just a sec." I dug around in my coat pocket and pulled out my chit bag. Then I slipped a twenty-chit piece from inside, balanced it on my thumbnail, whispered a few words to it, and flicked it into the air. It hung there for a few seconds, almost like it was deciding whether to fly or fall, before tumbling back down end over end. It plopped into the water with no resistance and sank into the deepness below.

"What was that for?" Saoirse asked.

"You know that myth about paying Charon to take you across the River Styx?"

"I think I remember something like that from school."

"Similar principle. You can summon the person who owes me a favor by paying a small tribute."

Saoirse balked. "Uh, who is this person ex…?"

The ocean beneath us began to tremble, the waves rising higher, growing rougher. Saoirse and I held onto each other and sank to our knees so we wouldn't get tossed around and separated. Together, we watched the water part forty feet in front of us, splitting in two as if someone was pulling a set of curtains aside. And from the black deeps of a gaping wound in the fabric of reality, that both belonged to the sea and did not belong anywhere, the bow of a great wooden ship punctured the edge of the realm, followed by the rest of its bulk. The ship pitched upward at a sharp angle before swinging down and crashing into the sea, sending a huge wall of water rushing toward us.

We were thrown almost ten feet into the air, still clinging to each other. Before we tumbled back to the sea below, landing with a dull, painful thud atop the surface. As the waters stilled around us, I quickly checked Saoirse for serious injuries, while she did the same for me. Both of us gave the other a quick nod, confirming we were a little battered and bruised, but not much worse for wear than we'd been before. Then, we shakily rose and stood in the shadow of the ornately carved ship with no sails, known to antiquity as *Scuabtuinne*.

Wave Sweeper.

At the bow, one foot on the railing, stood a tall, bulky man with a head of thick, curly black hair, an equally impressive beard, and piercing eyes of such a deep, dark green that they made you feel as if you could get lost inside them for all eternity, screaming for help to no avail. The man peered down at Saoirse and me with undisguised annoyance and extreme scrutiny, both of us looking foolish and meek under his gaze, bloody and beaten and so disheveled that not even a burger joint would allow us inside.

Finally, after a long moment of uncomfortable silence, the man shouted, "Vincent Whelan? Is that your dumb ass down there?"

In response to that unnecessary question, I glared up at

the man and flipped him off. Then I turned to Saoirse and said, "Allow me to introduce you to Manannán mac Lir. God of the Sea. Protector of Borders. Ferrier of Lost Souls. And absolutely incorrigible jerk. He's going to help us save Kinsale from obliteration."

CHAPTER FOURTEEN

Once Saoirse and I climbed aboard *Wave Sweeper* via a rather rickety rope ladder, Manannán whistled a high note, and the ship began to move in a direction I couldn't gauge. Not that it mattered much, since the Endless Sea never ended, and you had to cast portal spells to breach the veil between all the realms it touched. I got the sense Manannán only ordered the ship to move because he was accustomed to the rocking of a ship in motion. After all, he'd been sailing the waters of the various Otherworld realms—and on occasion, the Earthly oceans—for nigh on three thousand years.

Saoirse sank down onto the deck and leaned back against the mainmast, exhaustion digging deeper into the wrinkles on her face. "I know we're a little short on time, with the spell being cast late tonight," she said, "but please tell me we can take a break before we go gallivanting off for another leg of this paranormal adventure. I feel like I've been banging around in a cement mixer for the past two hours."

"Actually, that's another fun fact about the Endless Sea." I propped my arms on the railing and regarded the expanse of rippling blue water. "Time here is out of step with Earth. It passes a lot quicker. We've been here for, what, thirty minutes? Back on Earth, it's probably only been two or three."

Her tight expression melted into relief. "I'm going to ignore how weird that is and just be happy I don't have to spend the next half hour running away from svart...uh, dark elves."

Manannán, who'd been watching us speak as he lounged near the bow, perked up at Saoirse's words. "What's this about svartálfar?"

"We had a nasty fight with a group of them earlier," I answered, meandering closer to the sea god. "They're working for someone, identity unknown, who's planning to use a magic item of some power to cast a spell that'll wake a dormant enemy of the fae."

Manannán frowned. "Which enemy?"

"Don't know that either. We don't have a lot to go on, except the address of a potential base of operations." I waved my hand up and down, gesturing to him. "Which is why I called you here. I need to cash in my marker in exchange for a ride to the slip point in Tír na nÓg that coincides with the address."

Manannán looked less than impressed. He scratched his thick beard as he replied, "Shouldn't this be a matter you bring to Mab, if the threat is occurring in an Earthly domain she's claimed?"

"If I tell *her* about this"—I emphasized the pronoun because Mab was a lot more likely to pay attention to Manannán speaking her name aloud than a random human like Saoirse—"she'll send in the cavalry, and those assholes will trample my hometown and what little of civilization still lives in it."

"And?" Manannán lifted his hands, coaxing me for a better explanation. "Aren't there other cities under the protection of the queens you can immigrate to if yours gets 'trampled'? I do believe quite a few were set up to be safe havens for the humans and the scions of the Otherworld who, for some outlandish reason, chose to remain on Earth."

He didn't bother to stifle the reproving click of his tongue at my decision to stay in Kinsale after the collapse. And to a degree, his criticism was warranted. Almost half of all the paranormals who'd been living on Earth fled to the Otherworld during the purge or the war. Perfectly understandable, of course, given the way they were persecuted by so many world governments. But I had a good reason for staying put, and it wasn't a reason I sought to defend right now. Not while Saoirse was sitting a few paces away, watching this conversation with extreme interest.

"You'll forgive me, Manannán," I said, "if I consider a home something a person should seek to preserve. Yes, calling her and ratting out this troublemaker would be much easier than the track I'm currently on, but it would also sacrifice far too much I'm unwilling to so easily let slip through my fingers." I took four long strides toward the sea god, infringing on his personal space. He was a full head taller than me, but I met his steely gaze anyway and opposed it with one of my own. "She is the last option, not the first, when a gentle touch is required to favorably resolve a dangerous and delicate situation. You know that as well as I do."

Manannán crossed his arms and tilted his head from

side to side, considering my words. He could simply rat me out to Mab—he could contact her if he wanted, even though we were worlds away from Earth, and spill the beans faster than I could *attempt* to stop him—but she was no particular friend of his, or a direct authority. Manannán's role was one he'd chosen himself, to patrol the Endless Sea, scoop up lost souls, and send them to the afterlives where they belonged, and his powers were beholden to no one higher. He was a solitary being in every regard. And hell, he wasn't even fae.

Choosing to tell Mab the situation was something he would do only if he thought it would benefit him more than settling our score—that is, if he thought he could nab a favor from Mab in return for the intel. But Mab wasn't known to hand out favors for any old thing, because for her power to be at the behest of someone else in any way created a literal existential risk to the entire half of Tír na nÓg upon which the Unseelie Court was situated. So whatever you gave her had to be worth half a realm's weight in faerie gem chits.

"An enemy of the fae" was apparently too vague a notion to spur Mab's generosity, judging by Manannán's eventual shrug and reply of, "All right. Let's settle." In some ways, his response didn't surprise me. The fae had a lot of enemies, most of them too weak to be a true threat to the courts even if their full population numbered in the millions. Without more concrete information on the nature of the threat, Mab would likely be annoyed at any attempt from Manannán to procure a favor.

Good for Earth, so it works for me, I thought blithely.

Extending my hand to Manannán, I said, "Let's shake on it."

He took my proffered hand with his own substantially

larger one. "Vincent Whelan, do you agree to settle the debt between us if I safely convey you and your human companion to a specific location in Tír na nÓg, for the purpose of accessing a slip point?"

"Manannán mac Lir, I agree to settle the debt between us on the terms you have just stated."

There was a slight ripple in the air around our hands, followed by a faint tingling sensation under my skin. The sign of fulfillment conditions being added to a magic contract already in place.

I tugged my hand free as the sensation faded. "I'll get you the address."

Saoirse, who'd been paying attention like a dedicated pupil, opened her messenger bag and retrieved the ledger, turning it to the correct page. She offered it to Manannán. "It's the last entry on this page."

Manannán made a subtle motion with his chin, and the ledger slipped from Saoirse's hand and flew toward him. It stopped in front of his face and hovered in the air at eye level. He read the address a couple times, glanced to the side like he was calculating something, then whispered a few words I couldn't decipher, a spell in a language far more ancient than anything I knew. The spot on the page that contained the address faintly glowed blue, before wisps of energy rose off the paper like fog from damp earth and formed a series of numbers written in the standard numeral set used in the faerie courts.

"That's where you need to go in Tír na nÓg," Manannán said.

I committed the coordinates to memory before the foggy numbers dissipated into faint curls of mist, carried off by the light wind. "I assume if you're telling me the location, you aren't going to personally accompany us?"

"No offense, but I'm wasting my time speaking to you as it is, Whelan." He tucked his hands into the pockets of his loose-fitting tunic shirt. "The percentage of souls getting lost in the sea has increased drastically in recent years thanks to the human war. I've got my work cut out for me. I can sense dozens of new arrivals floating aimlessly right now, waiting for my help. So no, I will not go roaming around Tír na nÓg with you, though I'm sure your lovely lady friend would make a fantastic traveling companion."

Saoirse made a choking noise, but quickly covered it with a fake cough.

Manannán shot Saoirse a wink. "Just pointing out the obvious."

I scowled at him. "She's too young for a bag of bones like you."

"And you're too young to speak to a god that way."

"Too young, maybe," I muttered, "but not too low on the hierarchy."

Manannán smirked. "Watch yourself, Whelan," he said in a low voice, too soft for Saoirse to parse, "you can't claim a place in the court if you don't also claim the responsibilities that come with it. Best not to tempt fate, if you do indeed value your quaint little human station as much as you say."

"I do all my best work when tempting fate," I shot back.

"And in so doing, you ignore what fate portends."

I snorted. "Fate can go fuck itself. I don't care—"

"Um, excuse me," Saoirse said, using the mainmast to hoist herself to her feet, "as fascinating as it is to watch you two verbally duke it out in shady, threatening whispers, I think Vince and I should be getting on with our mission." She shook her messenger bag, indicating the contents, then gestured to her torn and wrinkled cocktail dress. "Do you perhaps have a room, er, cabin, I can use to change?" She paused. "Free of charge, and *favors*, that is?"

Manannán threw his head back and laughed. "Of course. I won't haggle with you over something so slight. I'm not one of those pesky lesser fae." He pointed to a door near the stern that must've led to one of the few cabins on the ship. "You can use my quarters. Just don't touch anything 'mystical.' Like the desk. Or the chairs."

Saoirse furrowed her brows. "Mystical chairs?" she murmured, as she skirted around the mast and shuffled toward the door. "What's next, a mystical spork?"

I'd have loved to tell her there was probably one of those too, somewhere in the Otherworld, but she disappeared through the door and slammed it shut behind her before I had the chance to *really* screw with her understanding of the universe. Instead, I said to Manannán, "What mode of transportation are we taking, if not your fancy boat here?"

"I'm calling in a long-time associate to give you a ride." A wide grin stretched across his face. "You ever ridden in a chariot, Whelan?"

"I can't say I've had the pleasure." I dredged up my minimal knowledge about the sea god's mythos and sifted through it, trying to remember which of Manannán's "associates" used a chariot as a primary mode of transportation. No one came to mind, but yet again, I had that itch in the back of my head, a faint notion I had a childhood memory that contained the exact knowledge I sought. But I couldn't quite reach through the haze of what time and intention had weathered away in order to find it.

"First time for everything." Manannán snickered as he raised his hand, a misty blue aura spiraling up his arm to the tips of his fingers. He snapped his fingers, and a small sphere of bright blue light with a brilliant tail, resembling a comet, shot up into the air like a rocket to the stars. Higher and higher and higher still, until it pierced the sky and soared off into the endless black in which the billions of realms of the Otherworld were suspended. "There. My associate will receive that message momentarily, and then he'll make his way here forthwith. Shouldn't be too long a wait."

The door to the captain's cabin creaked open, and Saoirse emerged wearing a typical outfit of jeans, boots, and a creased leather jacket I'm pretty sure she owned seven years ago. She hoisted the messenger bag over her shoulder as she crossed the deck, eying the ledger that was still floating near Manannán's head. "Can I have that back?"

"Oh, certainly." The notebook dropped into Manannán's hand, and he tossed it Saoirse's way.

She caught it and tucked it into its space inside her bag. "Any news on our ride out of here?"

"If you look up," said the sea god with a touch of amusement, "you will see your 'ride' descending through the heavens to join us."

Saoirse and I peered up at the dark sky, gazes tracking the span of the horizon in search of the mysterious associate promised to ferry us to the slip point. At first, I didn't notice anything new, even with my heightened vision scrutinizing each prominent feature in the celestial dome. But then I caught a flicker of light in my periphery, and I craned my neck to find a white streak breaking away from the diffuse glow of a distant cosmic body.

It dove through the atmosphere above the sea, briefly flaring red as the friction nearly caught it on fire. Some thousands of feet above us, the object began to slow, and as it hurtled toward the boat, a recognizable form emerged from what had been an amorphous blur. It was a white horse with a long, silver mane, decked out in golden armor and hooked to an ornate wooden chariot lined with gold accents.

Suddenly, that half-forgotten memory tickling Manannán's taunt grew crystal clear.

"Énbarr of the Flowing Mane," I murmured aloud.

"Bah!" Manannán spat. "You ruined my introduction. I was going to impress the lady with a rousing announcement in my suave, rumbling bass."

"I'm impressed enough already," Saoirse said absently, staring in awe at the horse-drawn chariot falling through the sky. "I feel like I'm in a fairy tale."

Énbarr broke off from his sharp descent as he neared the ship and came in at a shallower angle, swooping around us four times before he finally slowed enough to trot to a graceful stop atop the water. The chariot's wheels softly kissed the surface behind him. At the sight of the horse's smooth landing, Manannán whistled again, a low note this time, and the power that was driving the ship through the sea immediately cut out, bringing us to a halt with the mainmast in line with the horse standing off to the starboard side. The sea god then marched over to the railing and shouted something in that same ancient language I didn't know.

Énbarr didn't speak, but I swore he gave me a critical look with his big, black eyes after Manannán finished his clipped explanation of what he needed. The horse snorted and gestured with his head toward the chariot, urging his new passengers to climb on. Saoirse and I exchanged wary glances, her questioning whether riding a chariot pulled by a magic horse was a good idea, me questioning whether riding a chariot pulled by a magic horse that didn't like me was a good idea.

Manannán wasn't offering us any other options, however, so I shrugged and motioned to the rope ladder we'd used earlier. Saoirse climbed down first. I waited on the deck, steadying the ladder, as she descended toward the surface of the ocean.

As soon as Saoirse was out of earshot, Manannán, looming just behind me, said quietly, "You better make sure your courtly cohorts don't catch wind of the fact the svartálfar have grown brazen enough to use iron against the fae." He pointed a finger at the prominent iron burn on my arm, visible through my torn sleeves. "Some fool bringing Mab's wrath down on a human city is one thing, but there's been growing unrest on this side of the veil as well since the queens' decision to invade Earth. Certain creatures with dark agendas encroaching on court lands, raiding villages, carrying out assassinations. Those left behind to manage the courts are on a hair trigger as a result. I do not recommend you feed that fire."

"You don't care if the queens raze the Earth," I retorted, "so why should I care if something nasty leaves a few scratches on Tír na nÓg?"

Manannán sent me a chilly look. "Don't act daft, boy. It doesn't suit you. You know precisely why one is more important than the other." He kept up the hard glare for a second longer, then let out a faint sigh. "Look, I understand why your loyalties lie where they do, why you prefer to live where you do, but spite is not a good reason to recklessly risk major damage to the stability of the faerie courts. And you know it. So act as if you know it, Vincent Whelan, if for no other reason than maintaining the ethics you lay claim to."

A blush crept up my neck, but I beat it back with a deep glower, which I cast Manannán's way. "I didn't ask to play a pivotal role in this game."

"No one does." He made a sweeping motion, dismissing me from his boat. "That's why so many pieces on the board get broken."

Unease grew like a sinkhole in my stomach. Because Manannán's face had now morphed into that of a true god, the knowledge of ages, a heavy, bloody burden, pooling in the depths of his dark green eyes, his gaze so intense that it physically hurt, almost like it was flaying my skin, one paper-thin layer at a time.

I swung over the railing and climbed down the ladder as quickly as I could without slipping and falling on my ass, to the amusement of Saoirse and the goddamn horse. Still, Manannán's disconcerting eyes followed me with laser-like precision, boring into the back of my head, setting off goose bumps across my skin. Until I clambered onto the chariot next to Saoirse, and Énbarr, without waiting for a signal, shot off with the two of us in tow across the Endless Sea.

Is it just my imagination, I wondered as I clung to the chariot for dear life, *or am I missing a bigger picture here?*

CHAPTER FIFTEEN

I WAS BARELY ABLE TO BABBLE THE COORDINATES TO ÉNBARR over the rushing wind before the fabric of reality split before us. The chariot hurtled away from the Endless Sea and onto rolling hills of golden grass that suddenly spun into view from nowhere. We landed with nary a bump, the chariot imbued with magic that had made it a comfortable vehicle for many an ancient god and other powerful people of myth and legend. The wheels glided along through the tall grass, almost as if it wasn't touching the ground, and once I got a grip on the rim, I was able to heave myself into a half-crouch and observe the luscious landscape passing by.

Saoirse remained on her knees, clutching the top of the chariot, face pressed against a front panel, until I nudged her with my foot. She gave me a nervous look when I tilted my chin up, urging her to stand along with me. But she complied nonetheless, the rusty but deep-rooted trust between us quelling her fears. When she finally peeked over the rim at the new world around us, she gasped, and her gaze darted every direction, drinking in the strange, unearthly sights of Tír na nÓg, land of the faeries.

The golden, rolling hills stretched for miles in all directions, intersected by dense woodland populated with trees taller than any Sequoia. The trunks of these enormous wooden beasts were twisted in ways that some would call gnarled, gargantuan branches hanging both low and high, broad and long enough to build upon. There were structures in some of them, tree houses of a sort humans could never construct, built not from wood or plastic or stone, but from the smaller offshoots of the branches themselves, grown into shapes, the gaps filled with leaves and moss, and the roofs made of tightly woven vines.

Beyond these structures, in the deeps of the woodland, bound in shadow, were intermittently flashing lights of all colors. Some were mere flickers, tiny as bugs, while others illuminated the outlines of hulking creatures that prowled the land in search of needs like food and drink and worthy adversaries. Farther in still were things you couldn't see, but *feel*, eyes as old as time cutting through the black to watch everything that passed through the golden fields beyond. Even Saoirse could feel these creatures watching her, human as she was. Their hawk-like stares tickled that primal fear that existed in the genetic memories of all things.

"My god," Saoirse said, her words nearly lost to the wind. "Did I fall asleep?"

"The better question is," I replied, "could you dream up something so fantastical?"

She shook her head, a wry smile tugging at her lips. "Good point. I'm not this creative."

"This is where they live, the faeries." I leaned closer to her ear so she could hear me better. "We're currently in the domain of the Seelie Court, the Land of Eternal Summer and Bloom, ruled by you-know-who."

Saoirse nibbled on her lip. "The queen whose name starts with a *T*? I assume she can hear us when we say her name too?"

"See? You're learning." I winked at her in a far less flirty way than Manannán had. "The coordinates for the slip point are here somewhere, so we won't have to go through Unseelie territory, thank goodness."

"Unseelie are the winter faeries, yeah?" Saoirse asked. "And your mother is one?"

I got an awful metallic taste in my mouth just from hearing the word "mother," but I threw on a smile and nodded anyway because Saoirse didn't mean anything by the question. She didn't know about my early childhood. No one on Earth did except my father, and he was dead.

"The Unseelie are aligned with winter, yes," I replied, "like the Seelie are with summer, but the dichotomies are a bit more nuanced than a seasonal contrast. Different types of faeries are allied with each court, due to inherent differences in their natures. It's like…a bunch of complicated spiritual mumbo jumbo. Don't worry too much about it."

Énbarr took a sharp turn that somehow didn't phase the chariot—because who cared about the laws of physics in the Otherworld, right?—and carried us onto a narrow cobblestone road that curved around the hills and the borders of the hulking woods. One such curve took us within thirty feet of the clear-cut edge of a small orchard tucked into the valley between two tall hills. In this orchard, a thousand-strong swarm of tiny pixies were viciously tearing into each other in an attempt to steal the most oblong blue fruits from whatever trees were growing there. The ground below the trees was littered with itty-bitty dismembered body parts. And splattered with blood. Lots of blood.

"Uh…" Saoirse said. "Is that normal?"

"I regret to inform you that absolutely nothing in this realm will strike you as normal."

"Still"—the wariness was creeping back into her voice—"the gore kind of ruins the scenery."

We sailed around the base of a hill, which blocked the orchard from view.

"There," I said, "scenery restored."

Saoirse gave me a skeptical look.

"Or not."

Énbarr carried us along the cobblestone road for the better part of an hour before he veered off to the right and cut through a wide field of mixed gold and green grass nearly five feet tall. In the center of this field, the grass had been sheared to the earth with either a scythe or a spell in a circle roughly forty feet in diameter. Within the circle stood several rings of dense bushes with prickly leaves, dotted with lush red berries I was pretty sure were poisonous.

The horse jumped the outer ring of the bushes, carrying the chariot over them in a sharp arc, and landed inside the circle, then took us around the perimeter until we reached the spot that must've corresponded to the coordinates I'd given him. He brought the chariot to a halt, turned his head toward the second ring of bushes a few feet to the left, and snorted to indicate a particular bush. I assumed that meant we should stand close to that bush in order to access the desired slip point.

Saoirse was stumbling out of the chariot before I could offer her any help, a little wobbly from the wild ride and the strange sights. I hopped off after her and skirted around the chariot, coming to stand between Énbarr and the designated bush. "Thanks for the ride," I said to him. "That's all we needed, so you can fly away home now. Or back to whatever realm you were in before." Énbarr was associated with numerous figures from myth, so he could've been accompanying any of them for various tasks. Or maybe he'd simply been on vacation in some realm with lots of fields where magical horses and unicorns like to frolic. Who knew?

Énbarr jerked his head to toss a loose piece of his silvery mane away from his eye, and proceeded to shoot me the most annoyed expression a horse could possibly produce. As if I'd totally ruined his day by requesting a lift. He let out one final dismissive snort before he loped off over the outer ring of bushes, nearly whacking me in the face with one of the chariot wheels in the process. And then he was gone, barreling off across the hills so fast he was nothing but a white blur glinting with flecks of gold under the bright light of the Seelie Court's eternal day.

"And you thought I had an attitude," I said to Saoirse.

"You *do* have an attitude," she replied. "The horse just has a worse one."

I feigned offense.

She laughed. "Okay, back to reality—or fairyland. Where exactly are we?"

"No clue. Probably a sacred garden that belongs to a short-tempered faerie with a big club who'll kill us if they see us standing among the holy fruit."

"Please tell me that's a joke," Saoirse sputtered.

"It is and it isn't," I replied like a cryptic asshat. "No worries though. We won't be here long enough for our trespassing to matter either way." I indicated the bush. "We need to stand there. I'll open the slip portal, we'll slide on through, and we should end up somewhere in the vicinity of the house at the ledger address."

"What if we end up *in* the house?" she asked, trudging over to the bush.

"Then someone's going to have uninvited dinner guests." I tugged on her bag strap. "Might want to have your gun locked and loaded. Just in case."

"What about you?" She took her position in front of the bush as she dug her gun out from the bottom of the bag.

"What *about* me?" I sauntered up next to her. "I don't carry a gun anymore."

"I was referring to the weapon you do use. Your magic? You looked a little bushed at the tail end of that fight with the dark elves."

"Oh, that." I absently tugged at my torn sleeve. "My magic got overexcited because I pushed it too hard, and it's a struggle to restrain it."

She frowned. "What do you mean by 'overexcited'?"

I almost tried to dismiss the question, but this was Saoirse. If I tried to hold too many things back from her, particularly when she knew something was amiss, she'd dig up the skeletons whether I gave her a shovel or not. "Faerie magic, particularly Unseelie magic, is wild and pernicious, so much so that it almost seems to have a mind of its own. By using glamours, I suppress its nature, but when I access a significant amount of power and utilize it for combat, that nature begins to fight the suppression, urging me to strip my glamours away entirely and apply its full strength. It gets extremely agitated if I get hurt by iron, and extremely aggressive if I injure or kill someone."

Saoirse's mouth dropped open, releasing a soundless, "Oh."

"Anyway," I continued in a blatant attempt to steer us out of awkward territory, "my magic has calmed since the fight with the elves ended. Plus, being in Tír na nÓg, even on the Seelie side, is soothing like a balm. Feels like home."

"Got it. So you're good if we get into another brawl?"

"Until they break out the iron, yeah." I cringed. "Let's hope this house doesn't have a fireplace."

"Or security bars on the windows."

"That too." I held up my arms. "Same deal as last time. Hang on tight."

Saoirse stepped closer and wrapped her arms around my waist. "Out of remote—and probably ill-fated—curiosity, what happens if I let go while we're flying through that big abyss?"

"Um, well…to be honest, I'm not entirely sure. Some people say you get spit out in a random realm. Some people say you get lost in the void forever. I've never been inclined to test which outcome is the true one."

"They both sound awful, so I'm not sure it matters." She pressed herself harder against my chest, arms locked across my back. "Okay, ready as I'll ever be to travel in the most embarrassing manner in the multiverse."

I chuckled. "It's only embarrassing because you can't make a portal yourself. But if you ever find yourself wanting to travel solo to this land of milk and honey and heinous creatures that have a taste for human flesh, get thee to a witch or wizard and buy a portal talisman."

"They sell those?"

"Absolutely. Before the collapse, certain magicless humans 'in the know' would occasionally travel to the Otherworld for various reasons. Not as common now because of the ill will between the humans and…everyone else, but I'm sure some of the practitioners in Kinsale still have a few talismans in stock. *If* you'd like to have one, for emergencies, and not for sightseeing." I mocked a chastising expression, eyebrows furrowed to the point of silliness. "The Otherworld is not for day trips and picnics, you know, Lieutenant. Unless you fancy becoming the food."

She pinched my back with her short but surprisingly sharp nails. "Oh, shut up. You knowing more than me about the paranormal doesn't make you my teacher. It makes you a confidential informant."

I let out a loud, dramatic gasp. "Is that all I am to you now? I'm hurt."

"Suck it up, buttercup, and let's get on the ball. We've got an asshole with a harp to stop."

I snickered. "Boy, this policing thing sure has gotten weird in recent years."

"Tell me about it."

I wrapped one of my arms around Saoirse and summoned up the memory of the spell for a slip portal, forming another frosty circle on the ground beneath us. This one wasn't nearly as large or complex as the directed portal circle I'd used in Kinsale, which hopefully meant its presence wouldn't anger whoever's grass I was currently killing with subzero temperatures. Whispering out the syllables of the invocation in quick succession, I felt the veil between realms fluttering with a light resistance, as it always did from the Otherworld side. The barrier found it "distasteful" that one would seek to move from a realm of epic power to a mundane place of minimal magic like Earth.

As the final word rolled off my tongue, and the veil split at last to allow us through, Saoirse spoke to calm her budding nerves: "Say, I forgot to ask, what exactly did that sea god guy owe you a favor for anyway?"

"Oh," I replied as we began to slip through the ground into the endless void, "some years back, I helped Manannán resolve a dispute over his ship. Nothing big. It just involved some redcap pirates, a banshee thief, and a yeti with an RPG launcher."

"Wait, *what*?"

It was too late for me to answer. Our heads dropped under the cusp of the circle, and we careened off once more through the blackness, back toward Earth, back toward the battle for Kinsale, back toward our adversary who was preparing to cast a spell with a magic harp and a heaping helping of conceit that would incur the wrath of the wrong kind of fae.

It was fine though. I could always tell the yeti story later.

CHAPTER SIXTEEN

Iron lay before me. In the form of a dismantled wrought iron fence that someone had stacked in sections against the wall of the shed where Saoirse and I popped into existence. I stifled a warbling wail of terror at the sight of enough iron to cut me into a pile of smoking pieces and let out a faint squeak instead, which alerted Saoirse to a problem. She released me and whipped around, gun at the ready, expecting an enemy, only to find a wall and a bunch of inanimate metal pieces.

"Sorry," I whispered. "I wasn't expecting that."

Saoirse glanced at me, eyebrow raised. "Iron, I'm guessing?"

"Yeah, you know that innate fear of the dark all humans have? Iron is that fear for fae."

"Oh, well, don't worry." She patted my shoulder. "I'll protect you from the mean old fence."

"You're hilarious." I examined the shed and found the

door to my right. "Anyway, I'm guessing we're in the back yard of the correct property. Let's see if we can sneak a peek of what we're up against."

The two of us made our way to the door as quietly as possible. The shed was an obstacle course, strewn with toolboxes and lawn care equipment, wrenches and hammers hanging from the walls by nails driven into the wood. Every step I took, I feared making a loud noise by putting pressure on a warped floorboard or nudging the wrong object with my elbow. And Saoirse, with her human sight so weak in the dark, must have had it far worse. But we both reached the door without tripping and causing a ruckus that would give us away to anyone guarding the property. Then we carefully peered through the tiny gap between the double doors, one of them left open a fraction of an inch.

Beyond the shed was a modest yard covered in dead, damp grass that led to the two-story house I'd expected. The house had been painted a light blue before the collapse, but years of hard weather had chipped away at the paint, and it was now a faded white and peeling in places. The windows on the back side of the house were all intact, the ones on the ground floor shuttered, the ones on the top floor offering no view of the interior thanks to pulled curtains. Through those curtains and shutters, I spotted no light sources, nor did I hear any movement inside, even when I focused my heightened hearing to catch the softest of sounds.

"See anything?" Saoirse all but mouthed close to my ear.

I shook my head. "No activity at all. There's no one above ground."

"Maybe the basement?"

The lone basement window, too narrow for either of us to slip through, was boarded up.

"There's one more thing I can check," I said, and this time went on the hunt for any traces of magic. I scoured the house from the flagging antenna that had long lost its usefulness all the way down to the faux-brick skirt that lined the base of the home, the veneer heavily eroded in places from the continual battering of heavy rains and snows. It was always difficult to sense magic through the earth, something about ley lines and the flow of natural energy. But I pushed the spiritual sensory organ that let me detect magic as hard as I could without breaking it, steady gaze on the basement, willing any hints of our enemies to trip my alarms.

Just when I was about to give up and declare the house a bust, nothing but another laborious stop on our long road to solving this mystery, I caught the most tenuous wisp of magic emanating from one side of the basement. I couldn't determine its purpose or its origin, but there it was, plain as day: a sign that someone with magic in their bones was in the house, or had been recently.

I gave Saoirse the hand signal that meant, *Follow my lead*, threw a rudimentary veil over us both, and opened the shed door wide enough to slip through. To cross the yard, I had to take a roundabout path so I didn't wind up splashing my way through the massive puddles and announcing my approach to anyone within five blocks. Saoirse trailed me, stepping where I stepped so we didn't leave two sets of prints in the mud, and the ones we did leave were indecipherable. We crept up to the back wall of the house and slid along the siding until we reached the small wooden deck that led to the back—

I threw up my arm so Saoirse couldn't pass me on the deck

steps as my mind screamed *DANGER* so loudly it echoed from ear to ear. For a long moment, I couldn't figure out what the heck had tripped my senses. I slowly rolled my eyes, taking in the fenced yard again, the shed in one corner, the dark and cloudy sky above, the roof of the house with its missing shingles, the faded siding, cracked in places, the back door, the deck... *That's it.*

Dropping my attention to the steps beneath me, I saw more clearly what my peripheral vision had noticed: a tripwire stretched across the second step from the top, placed exactly where someone's shoe would snag it as they were ascending. I pointed it out to Saoirse, and we both tracked it to a grenade taped to one of the deck's support posts and largely hidden by the crisscrossing diagonal skirt.

Saoirse, wearing a perturbed frown, mouthed, *The house is a trap.*

I replied in kind, *And a warning bell.*

Gingerly stepping over the tripwire, I padded across the deck, on alert for any more booby traps. I figured the back door was also rigged to blow the moment someone opened it, so I ignored it for the time being. I climbed onto the deck railing where it connected to the exterior wall, and shook the kinks out of my muscles as I gauged the amount of strength I'd need to reach my destination. Next, I jumped straight up to the second-story window above the deck and grasped the sill.

The greater distance between Saoirse and me strained the construct of the veil. I pushed more energy into it to keep it stable as I reached up, stuck my hand through the torn screen, and pushed on the window.

The window was locked. I gave it a glower and threw a bolt of energy at it. Then it wasn't locked anymore. So I opened it, thankfully without making enough noise to wake the dead, and clambered through the ragged hole in the screen that snagged at my coat and somehow managed to reopen the cut on my ear, hot blood once again running down my neck. I made it into the upper-story bedroom, however, and didn't even knock over the dresser under the window. *That counts as a win, right?*

Once I was situated and had given the room a quick scan to make sure no svartálfar were hiding in the closet or under the bed, I looked down at Saoirse and gave her the wait signal. In an eerily similar situation to my awful trip to Walter Johnson's house, I tiptoed out of the bedroom and made my way down to the first floor of a house I knew to be under the control of an enemy. But I didn't run face first into any enemies this time, nor did they sneak up behind me like the ghouls. The kitchen and living room were unoccupied, all the doors on the ground floor fully closed.

Still, I approached the back door with trepidation, eyes and ears on the lookout for any creatures hiding behind the furniture or in dark corners, waiting to lunge and rip my throat out. I found the back door rigged like I'd thought it'd be, but the setup was as basic as the trap on the deck steps. Just two grenades taped to the door and a wire attached to the bottom of the doorframe, so that when you opened the door, it would pull the pins, and *boom*. No more door. And a nasty surprise for anyone walking in.

Of course, the blast wouldn't take down a paranormal, not even a human practitioner, but that wasn't the point. The grenades were merely meant to warn someone about an intruder on the premises.

I disabled the booby trap and opened the door.

Saoirse was waiting on the other side, foot tapping impatiently.

Neither of us spoke as we proceeded down the hall, to the door I wagered led to the basement. Since this door was almost certainly rigged to blow as well, I had to figure out a new way around the trap, because there was no alternate entry point to the basement. My solution wasn't elegant, but it was effective: I opened the door the tiniest fraction, giving me a line of sight to the wire. Then I stuck my finger into the gap, siphoned a small amount of magic energy to the tip of my finger, and extended that energy forward like a blade. The "blade" sheared through the wire, and the two ends fell away.

Nothing went kaboom, and I didn't die. So far, so good.

I pushed the door all the way open, revealing the steep, rickety stairs leading to the basement. I turned to Saoirse, who'd been loitering behind me, and mouthed, *Stay alert. Possible ambush.*

She nodded, took a SWAT stance, both hands on her gun, and replied, *Ready.*

The trip down the stairs was filled with faint squeaks, tense pauses, and the occasional collision, where Saoirse bumped into me because she couldn't see where she was going. Strangely, even *I* could barely see in the darkness of the basement, despite my faerie senses. It was as if the air literally teemed with black ink. It wasn't until I stepped off the stairs and pivoted around to the side of the basement where I'd caught the faint magic signature that I realized the dense shadow was part of yet another trap.

There was a thick metal door in the wall that didn't match the rest of the basement. A new addition. And before that door was a minefield of tripwire grenades, visible to me only because I knew where to look for the explosives, black lumps protruding from the walls and the ceiling joists. I couldn't see the actual wires. The low-power murk spell etched into the doorframe ensured that even the most heightened paranormal senses wouldn't be able to cut through the darkness.

"Damn," I whispered.

Saoirse shuffled closer to me and said into my ear, "What is it?"

I explained.

She worried her lip. "Can you disable the spell?"

"Without alerting the caster? Doubtful. They'll sense the dissipation of their magic. I might be able to subvert it though, if I can get closer."

"Why do you need to be closer?"

"Because spells also tend to have built-in 'alarms' that signal the caster if they're being tampered with. You have to stifle them quickly. But the farther you are from the ward you're trying to manipulate, the greater the delay between you giving your magic energy instructions and your energy responding to those instructions."

"Crap. So what do we do? You have to get past the tripwires to get *closer*."

"You stand way back there"—I pointed to the other end of the basement—"while I make like a contortionist and climb through the wires."

"You just said you can't see them."

"I can't." I stripped off my coat and folded it up, offering it to her. "But I *can* see the grenades, and I have a rough grasp of trigonometry. I can approximate where the wires are."

She snatched the coat from me, scowling. "You're going to blow yourself up."

"Nah. I can throw up a shield. The bigger problem is alerting whoever's at the end of the tunnel behind that door."

"Where do you think it goes?" She tucked my coat under one arm and gripped her gun with both hands again. "Another house in the neighborhood?"

I gave her a thin smile. "Probably cuts under the road to the house across the street. I'm thinking the harp was delivered here, then carried along through the tunnel to the *real* base of operations, with a number of goons, at least one of whom was a magic practitioner, leaving booby traps in their wake. That way, if someone tracked the harp here…"

"They'd hit a trap, causing a ruckus," Saoirse picked up, "which would alert everyone across the street to the fact they'd been found out. And while the person or persons in this house recovered from the grenade blast and tried to avoid setting off more, all the bad guys would grab or destroy any incriminating evidence in their real base, then rush out of the house and flee into the woods a few blocks north of here."

"Clever." I rubbed my gloved hands together as I eyed the literal minefield in front of me. "But not *that* clever."

"I don't know. This whole scheme stayed under wraps right up until the last minute." She felt all her pockets until she found her phone and covered the screen to diminish the glow as she checked the time. "It's quarter after two. The spell's supposed to be cast at three, the witching hour. Maybe whoever's running this gig just figured he wouldn't need a better-hidden base because no one would show up to stop him in time. A touch of arrogance, for sure, like you said, but considering how close to the wire we are"—she glanced at the minefield—"no pun intended, I don't think this guy overestimated himself by much. I mean, you only stumbled onto this whole operation because you were literally led into it by a third party. If that hadn't happened..."

"Yeah." I frowned. "That still rubs me the wrong way. I hate being played."

She chewed on the inside of her cheek. "Do you have any idea who might've wanted to drag you into this?"

"Not yet." I dropped the pitch of my voice. "But rest assured, I'll find out."

Saoirse dipped her head. "You should. I can't stand the idea of people being moved around like pieces in somebody's game."

"Me either. Which is precisely why I don't live among the fae."

She winced. "You think one of them hired that 'Tom' guy to trick you?"

"Oh, definitely. That's not up for debate. The real question is *which* faerie?" I rolled my shoulders and searched the walls and rafters for the nearest black shape that roughly equated to a grenade. "But that's a riddle we can solve after we save the day."

Saoirse backed into the farthest corner when I began my approach to the door. "Seriously, Vince, don't set one of those things off."

"I'm not making guarantees. You know how *guarantees* pan out for cops."

A brief silence. Then a sigh. "Right. Just get it over with."

CHAPTER SEVENTEEN

Like an art thief in a cat suit corkscrewing through a gallery of lasers, I bent and stretched and contorted my way across the minefield, sometimes coming within an inch of a tripwire, my skin sensing its presence in the darkness. At one point, halfway to the door, I lost my footing on a slick patch of concrete. I had to brace myself against a support beam, which caused me to inadvertently brush a wire with my ear. I froze. Waited for that disastrous telltale plink of a pin being pulled.

But it didn't come. I hadn't put enough pressure on the wire. *Lucky break, Whelan,* I thought as I breathed out a deep sigh of relief, heart still pounding against my ribs. Steadying myself, I ducked under the tricky wire and continued on.

When I passed the bulk of the grenades and emerged into a clear space in front of the door, I had the urge to jump up and cheer. But I couldn't. Because there was yet another trip-wire about six inches above my head. If I ever saw another tripwire grenade after tonight, I swore to all hells I was going to shove it down its owner's throat. The constant threat of being consumed by fire, my natural enemy, was grinding on my already frayed nerves, and my winter-tuned magic was grumbling about it too. It was almost worse than the threat of the barghest hanging over my head.

Which reminds me, that thing will track me down soon now that I'm back on Earth. Better hustle.

I shuffled up to the doorframe and crouched to examine the murk spell more closely. It was a basic construction designed to bend light in ways that would create the illusion of a dense black fog within a certain area. There were several ways to subvert the spell without breaking it, and I went with the easiest because it was also the quickest:

Shooting threads of my own magic energy into the glowing symbols on the wall, I strangled the alarm response before it could alert the caster by walling it off from the rest of the construction, then bridged a few of the spell's lines, added on to its symbols, to alter the layout of the murk in the basement. When I was done, the abnormal darkness behind me was missing a big chunk in the middle, revealing the tripwires and clearing the way for Saoirse to cross the room.

I threw a grin over my shoulder and beckoned for her to give me the pleasure of watching her relive her childhood gymnast days. She scowled the entire way through the minefield, and I swore she almost tripped one of the wires out of spite. She emerged on my end with a graceful tuck and roll that made my own efforts look like those of a stumbling drunk, and brushed her clothes off as she stood up. "You tell anyone about that," she muttered, "I'll have Kennedy raid your store."

If there ever was a better threat, I hadn't heard it.

After slipping my coat back on, I motioned for Saoirse to stand off to the side with her gun ready in case something jumped out at me when I opened the door. But besides a faint squeak of the hinges as I heaved the thick metal slab aside, there were no sounds on the other end. No rushing footsteps. No sizzling magic. No clicking guns. Just a wave of dank air that had been cooped up in the tunnel that cut underneath the road and led to our perp's home base.

I considered briefly whether a veiled ambush could be lying in wait in the darkness. But since human goons wouldn't be able to stop me regardless, and svartálfar were fans of direct confrontation, I doubted anyone would attack us in the tunnel. If anything, there'd be a large group of guards camped out on the other end, behind another metal door, on the lookout for intruders coming by way of their "secret entrance." In which case, Saoirse and I would simply have to come up with a strategy to sneak past them and not raise the alarm.

"We should be clear for now," I murmured to Saoirse, "but be prepared for resistance when we get to the other house. So close to the witching hour, they're probably on high alert. I expect security will be tight, particularly around the room where the spell is being prepared."

"Understood." She peered into the gaping void of the tunnel. "How are you planning to respond if they spot us?"

"I'm planning to make a grab for the harp and then run as fast as I can."

"Your brilliant tactics never cease to inspire, Vince."

"Oh, shut up. Like you have anything better."

"If we were up against humans, I would have about ten better plans."

"But we aren't, so you don't." I wagged my finger at her. "Which makes me the expert in this situation."

She faked a shudder. "What a terrifying thought."

"Fuck you too."

She smiled. "That reminds me, you owe me a date at a fancy restaurant."

"Excuse me?" I sputtered.

"Don't tell me you've forgotten." She stepped into the tunnel. "Two weeks before the exposure of the paranormals, I had a date with a really sexy firefighter named Ian. He took me to Armando's, that high-end Italian place that used to be on Plantain. Right after we got our appetizers, *you* burst in. You were covered in mud from a wrestling match you'd had at a construction site with that mob hitman, Vintano, after he tried to assassinate Deputy Mayor Murdock, whose protective detail you were on at the time. You ran up to our table, leaving muddy footprints all over the expensive carpet, grabbed my arm, yanked me out of my chair, and said, 'We have a conspiracy on our hands. The mayor's in danger! Let's go.' And I had to leave poor Ian all alone, and skip my dinner."

I racked my brain for a second, and came up with a memory that *somewhat* resembled her story. "Did I apologize?"

"Not really. You said you'd make it up to me later by taking me out to a fancy restaurant yourself." Her smile shifted into a grin. "I asked you if the only reason you came to me, instead of grabbing someone who was actually on duty, is because you were jealous of Ian, and you turned that delightful shade of pink you always do when embarrassed." She paused. "Yep. That's the one."

I slapped my hands over my flushing cheeks. "Shut up. I

wasn't jealous. I thought you'd be the best person to lead the team to hunt down Vintano's associates."

"Sure you did." She winked at me. "Anyway, you never made good on your promise. So you still owe me a date."

Clearing my throat, and willing my blush to fade, I replied, "Hate to break it to you, partner, but there's only one fancy restaurant left in this town, and Bismarck owns it."

"She might not after tonight. If it gets out that she's been defying the queens, her little business empire's going to crumble."

"That's true, but…"

"But nothing. You're going to take me out for dinner, one way or another. A debt is a debt. You're half faerie. You know that."

Saoirse had me there, so I just pouted at her.

"Oh, stop moping." She gestured into the tunnel with her gun. "Come on. Let's take down the mob lady and her mysterious associate."

"Fine," I said like a moody teenager, brushing past her. "But let me lead in case somebody throws a spell at us. You keep watch on our rear."

Together, we proceeded through the musty tunnel, which gradually narrowed as we neared the middle, to the point where we both had to bend our knees so our heads didn't drag along the damp earthen ceiling. The tunnel began to widen again as we neared the other end, where we found a door just like the one in the first basement. Except, for some reason, this door had a massive dent in the middle, bowed out toward us, like someone or something *very* strong had kicked it in a rage. That didn't bode well, but whatever had done it couldn't be more menacing than a barghest. Right?

At the door, Saoirse and I took up positions on either side of the dent and pressed our ears against the metal. My unglamoured hearing was more acute than hers, but I was pretty sure she could hear roughly as much activity as I could. The murmurs of fifteen to twenty people, some near, some far. The heavy, regular footsteps of soldiers marching up and down a tiled hallway. The clanging of metal on metal, high pitched and repetitive, like someone was using a hammer to bang on a sword…A blacksmith?

It sounded like the people on the other side of the door were preparing for war.

Saoirse and I pulled away from the door and exchanged nervous glances.

As quietly as I could, I turned the handle of the door and opened it the slightest crack, just enough for me to glimpse one direction down the hall. I expected enemies to charge me immediately, but whatever the people in the basement *were* preparing for, it had distracted them from assiduously guarding their secret entrance. So I was able to draw a solid mental image of the basement—or rather, the underground compound—and shut the door again before anyone noticed me peeping.

I then leaned close to Saoirse's ear and whispered, "The basement has been expanded into a kind of small military outpost. Barracks. Armory. Svartálfar crawling everywhere."

"You put one of those veil things over us earlier, right?" She made a gesture like she was throwing a sheet over her head. "Will that hide us from them?"

"No. Elves, both dark and common, can see through veils. It's a spiritual quirk. In fact…" I dispelled our veil. "There's no point in wasting the energy."

"So, what? We wait for an opening?" She bit her thumbnail. "Or cause a distraction?"

"Since we don't have much time before the spellcasting will get underway—and we can't predict if someone will come through this door in the meantime—I say we go with a distraction." I closed my eyes and reexamined my mental picture of the western half of the hall, searching for weaknesses in the construction. "There's some exposed water pipes bolted to the ceiling. They turn at the end of this hall and continue on to another section of the compound."

"You want to flood the place?" Saoirse scrunched her nose. "I'm not looking forward to more waterlogged shoes."

"Now it's your turn to suck it up." I wrung my hands, carefully siphoning a tiny amount of magic energy from my soul. I didn't want a big explosion of power that would alert every enemy to my presence in their midst. I wanted *just* enough to wreak the right amount of havoc. "This shouldn't take but a second. Watch."

Once the energy had gathered in my fingertips, I cracked the door open again and checked to see if the coast was clear. There were a couple dark elves loitering nearby, but they were speaking in harsh tones to each other and facing away from the door, preoccupied by whatever had the base in a *tizzy*. So I pointed two fingers at the nearest pipe. With a mental whisper that took a tad more effort than speaking an invocation aloud, I released the magic from beneath my skin as a nearly transparent white wisp and directed it into the pipe.

The moment it touched the water, folding into a compact seed of energy, it shot down the length of the pipe so fast the two elves standing beneath said pipe didn't sense a thing. The spell then took that sharp turn and kept going, and kept going, and kept going, until it hit yet another curve—which I knew because that was the condition under which I'd ordered it to explode.

A screech of tearing metal rebounded off the walls, followed by the unmistakable sound of water splashing across a tile floor. The two elves in sight of the door started, and took off to investigate. I shut the door as soon as they were gone and waited, hearing several more elves blow past, followed by a multitude of swears in a language I didn't speak. As soon as our stretch of the hall quieted, I opened the door a third time, wide enough to stick my head through, and quickly looked both ways. Clear.

I yanked the door halfway open, ushered Saoirse through, followed her, and then softly closed the door behind us. At her questioning eyebrow, I pointed to the opposite end of the hall from where I'd sent the spell. We hurriedly shuffled along, listening at every door, checking every nook for hostiles lying in wait, until we reached an intersection that branched off in two directions.

Saoirse mouthed, *Which way?*

It wasn't a question I had to think hard about. One end of the new hall was dead as a doormat. No lights. No people. No magic. Just two small doors across from each other I thought might've been supply closets. The other half of the hall was equally dark and seemingly deserted, no ceiling fixtures ever installed during the reno that added this new wing onto the basement complex. But magically, it was *alive*. Intense power practically bled from underneath a wooden door at the very end of the hall, coming in pounding waves that rattled my soul the way shockwaves rattled bones.

I jutted my thumb toward the door and mouthed back, *That way.*

Shuffling down the length of the hall, I signaled for Saoirse to prepare for a fight. The magic behind that door was considerably more powerful than anything we'd come across up to this point. Far beyond any dark elf. Far beyond most human practitioners. I could taste its vast complexity like blood on a razor's edge, a remnant of the first delicate incision of what would become a gaping wound carved through Earth's plane of existence. It was the sort of spell construction that was used to bridge *here* and *there* in a way that was both more stable and more devastating than any portal to the Otherworld.

If the spell behind that door was cast, it would leave in the veil between worlds a massive tear that would take centuries to heal, and would only ever scar. *A hole that all manner of dark and deadly things could use to access Earth.*

We reached the door. It wasn't warded, which I thought was either a gross oversight by an arrogant man or the telltale sign of a trap. But trap or not, Saoirse and I had to get into that room and recover the harp, or perhaps damage the spell construction—which would be a large and complicated circle—to the point that it couldn't be fixed before the witching hour. Since this particular spell was meant to be cast on the night of the full moon at three AM, sabotaging the circle meant the caster would have to wait an additional month. So even if we failed to recover the harp tonight, we could still win the day.

I would prefer to get the harp though. I wanted to win the war.

Ear against the door, I didn't hear anyone pacing the room, or even a slightly rapid heartbeat. If there was anyone in there, they were standing or sitting, perfectly calm and composed. I sent Saoirse a gun gesture, telling her to be ready to fire the second I whipped the door open. She nodded, stepped back to clear the door, and raised her weapon, finger hovering over the trigger.

Taking a deep breath, I put my magic on standby so I could raise a shield or shoot off an attack spell at a moment's notice. Then I gripped the doorknob. Exhaled. Turned the knob. Inhaled. Yanked the door open. Exhaled. Flooded my limbs with power. Inhaled—in a gasp.

The room beyond the door was bathed in a harsh golden glow from the single most intricate magic circle I'd ever seen. It was nearly thirty feet in diameter, strewn with symbols and shapes and lines whose arrangement exceeded every grasp of magic knowledge I possessed. At the center of the circle sat the harp, a proud instrument of weathered wood and silver strings, and it too was glowing, a soft white, revealing its true nature as an object of power.

But even if it hadn't been glowing, I would've recognized the harp for what it was. Because the second my gaze landed on it, a memory from my childhood flittered to the surface of my mind. I had *seen* that harp before, in a drawing in a book about the history of Tír na nÓg. A book borrowed from the Great Library of the Unseelie Court.

Daur Dá Bláo. Oak of Two Blossoms.

The harp of the Dagda, leader of the Tuatha Dé Danann.

CHAPTER EIGHTEEN

FIFTEEN HUNDRED YEARS AGO, THE LAST GREAT WAR BETWEEN the aes sídhe and Tuatha Dé Danann had ended in a resounding defeat for the latter after a brutal battle that raged for nearly four months straight and shook the very foundations of the Otherworld. The old rulers of Tír na nÓg, ancient and venerable, were then shunted aside for a new regime. But in a rare display of mercy, the faerie queens offered their longtime rivals an alternative to death: an endless sleep in Maige Mell, the Plain of Delight, a region deep in the heart of Tír na nÓg where no one was allowed to tread without explicit permission from a queen. And so off they'd gone to be laid to rest for eternity, and to fade in the collective memory, reduced to nothing but myths and legends.

Now someone was trying to wake them up.

Daur Dá Bláo. The instrument played by Úaithne, the Dagda's harper. It had been used as a call to arms during the many wars of the Tuatha Dé Danann and, according to the stories, had been played during that final battle, right up until the moment where Úaithne was slain by a powerful sídhe warrior from the Seelie Court. After that, the harp had fallen out of the old stories, slipped into obscurity, as so many things—and people—did once the reins of rule had been wrenched from their hands.

How it had also slipped through to Earth, I didn't know. And how someone had managed to locate it here after the collapse baffled me even more. But despite those lingering mysteries, the truth of the matter was clear. Someone intended to use the harp to break the spell that kept the Tuatha Dé Danann dormant in Maige Mell, which would once again pit the fae against their oldest enemies. And seeing as the bulk of the fae leadership was now based on Earth...it could mean a war on mortal soil.

Oh god.

"Judging by the look on your face, Vincent Whelan," said a voice that came from everywhere at once, "I'm going to assume you've figured out my play."

In the corner of the room, a veil so perfect that I couldn't have pulled it off with a century of practice dissolved into a lingering golden mist. Its dissolution revealed a man of average height and build, but whose red hair was streaked with gold and whose irises were green yet speckled with the same metallic aspect. He appeared no older than me, not a wrinkle on his face, but the way he stared into my eyes spoke of a lifetime so long and winding and storied, spoke of a power so far beyond my half-mortal comprehension, that my knees almost buckled in the spare second it took me to break eye contact.

Saoirse, affected worse than me, stumbled into the

doorframe. But she kept her brave face. "Who the hell are you?"

The man spared her a look, and smiled. "Lieutenant Daly. We met earlier, though I'm afraid I was wearing quite the glamour then, as a matter of practicality." Said glamour instantly coalesced around him, casting him as an ordinary man with brown hair and eyes. He wiped the glamour from existence a second later, as soon as Saoirse's sharp intake of breath met his ears. "See? You remember."

"From the auction." She frowned. "You said your name was something odd. Abar…Abarta?"

"Abarta?" I spat at the man, hands curling into fists, heart now pumping hard. "You're one of the Tuatha Dé Danann?" That was bad. Very, very bad. "You're supposed to be asleep in Maige Mell."

Quicker than I could blink, his cordial smile morphed into a sneer. "That's a nice way of saying the faerie queens tried to toss me into a catacomb to rot with the rest of my comrades."

"You agreed to that fate as part of your concessions for losing the final war."

Abarta barked out a laugh. "Agreed? You show your age, boy. Your ignorance." He rose, and the chair he'd been sitting in vanished into another puff of golden smoke. "We were still on the muddy, bloody battlefield when that 'agreement' was struck. The only reason our heads weren't lobbed off by the ice queen's blade is because her warmer counterpart convinced her that we might one day be of use to them, if some future issue in Tír na nÓg could be rectified by our continued existence. It was only the slightest compromise on the queens' end, the slightest risk, since they still held all the power and were unlikely to wane or be challenged in the ensuing centuries. But for us…for us, it was either an ignoble end, or a long-term *gambit*, depending on which of us you asked."

"So you're saying"—I struggled to grasp at the fraying ends of my thoughts, to stall Abarta until I could think of something, anything, to do to get Saoirse and myself out of this unwinnable conflict with a man who'd once been a god—"some of the Tuatha Dé Danann wanted to die for honor's sake, while others were still plotting a way to win the war, even when they were on their knees in the shadow of Mab's sword?"

Abarta didn't miss the fact I used her name out loud. He shot me a dark look, darker than the void between worlds, daring me to say it again. At which point I was sure he'd blow me away with a single spell. I'd be lucky if there were ashes left of me, this man's power was so much greater than my own.

"Keep going," he said in a false friendly tone that sent a shudder crawling down my spine, "you've figured out the gist of it, haven't you?"

"You, uh…" I swallowed, my mouth suddenly dry. Saoirse was visibly quaking. I realized that Abarta's magic was now rolling off him in waves of steam, cinders of his golden aura glittering in the air. Even mundane humans could feel the pressure of such magic in their souls. *What a fucking idiot I was, dragging Saoirse into a hornet's nest.*

Abarta took a step toward me, and I instinctively took a step back.

Amusement twinkled in his gold-flecked eyes. "Keep going, I said."

"After the agreement was struck, you somehow slipped free—"

"Not quite," he interrupted. "I wasn't in the lineup. I was already 'dead.'"

"You were playing dead, you mean," I said. "You were a trickster god, through and through, so you hid yourself among the fallen. But surely they checked to make sure—"

"Oh, sure they did," he said, enunciation sliding nearer to the hissing of a snake. "They sent the cleanup crew around to poke a few extra holes in the dead, just in case." He clapped his hands together, startling Saoirse and me, making us jump, making us look like scared little mice. "And when one came around to poke holes in me, I poked a few extra in him instead. And then I took his armor. And his face. And the rest of his skin too." You didn't even have to see the manic gleam in his eye to know he meant those statements literally. "And I walked right off the battlefield and hid among the fae. For years and years and years. Totally undetected."

"While the rest of your comrades went to sleep. Until you could secure their release, by finding Daur Dá Bláo and using it to break the spell." I bit my tongue until I tasted copper. "But that…" I took a shaky breath. "That sounds like the sort of plan you'd come up with in advance, as a contingency, not some half-assed scheme you'd make up after the fact, after the battle was lost."

He shrugged. "What can I say? Some among us were simply not willing to lose to the aes sídhe, even if we had to play a long game to win. They invaded our home. Took our lands." His voice grew into an ear-breaking rumble. "Tír na nÓg belonged to us!"

Abarta stepped forward again, and despite my best efforts, my shaking legs made me step backward again. But I was drawing close to the wall behind me. Soon, there'd be nowhere to go.

Eyes alight with satisfaction, he dropped his voice to a normal volume. "And it will belong to us once more." He made a sweeping gesture to the magic circle, to the harp sitting within. "The new war begins tonight, when the chords of Daur Dá Bláo once again call the Tuatha Dé Danann to war."

"Why are you doing this now?" I said. "You've had fifteen hundred years to recover the harp."

"Can you really not think of a reason?" He pointed to the ceiling, but the ceiling wasn't the implication. It was the emptiness of the house above. The lack of people left living in what had once been a home. The grievous results of humanity's last war.

It came to me then. "The forces of the fae are split between Earth and Tír na nÓg. If you awaken the Tuatha Dé Danann, they can overrun the courts in one realm before the greater forces in this world, spread far and wide across the globe, can muster an organized response to the threat." I gritted my teeth, fists clenched so hard my gloves were threatening to tear. "Most of the faeries still living in Tír na nÓg are lesser fae civilians."

"Yes, I am aware," Abarta replied with no emotion whatsoever. "But the land on which they live is not theirs to live on, the resources not theirs to use. So they can flee and leave my realm and crawl back into the hole they came from, or they can stay and fight and die. Their choice."

"I won't defend the imperialist history of the fae." I met his gaze straight on this time, even though my very soul quivered beneath its weight. *Stand firm, Whelan. Stand firm.* "But that does not justify the mass slaughter of civilians, any more than the humans were justified in committing genocide against the paranormals when they discovered we had 'infiltrated' their society."

"Ha!" Abarta shook his head and gave me a pitying look. "Justification is irrelevant when hatred fuels the fire of war. The humans were always destined to slaughter the nonhumans the second they found out you were their neighbors, their *relatives*. They fear everything they don't understand, hate everything they fear, and destroy everything they hate— because it's their nature. Same as you have a faerie nature, hiding behind that pathetic glamour. Same as I have the nature of my kind."

"You generalize too much." Anger spiking, I racked my brain for some semblance of a plan before I did something stupid and got myself killed. *There's got to be a way out of this. Some way to stall or distract him long enough to escape.* "Even among the fae, spiritual natures are individualized. Not all humans are cruel to those they don't understand."

"Like her, you mean?" Abarta motioned to Saoirse, and for one terrible moment, I thought he was going to kill her where she stood. But the sensation of impending doom slid past, and Abarta continued, "I don't disagree with you, Whelan. But individual will only matters insomuch as there are enough dissenting views to change the course of a species' natural tendencies. And unfortunately for your poor little world, there were not. So the 'paranormals' were burned at the stake, and the humans were burned in the bomb blasts."

Pride wriggled across his face, settling deep inside his smile. "Exactly as planned."

I had the sudden and unmistakable sensation of being disemboweled, all my organs spilling out and sloshing on the floor, so overwhelming that I glanced down to see if it had actually happened. But it hadn't. The feeling was simply my entire worldview crumbling to dust, leaving nothing its in wake but an absolute and awful emptiness. "What do you mean?"

Abarta took yet another step toward me, and I was so unsettled, I stumbled two steps back. The strength of the pity in his voice grew stronger with each word he spoke. "Tell me, Whelan, what sparked the purge that haunts you all so much? What alerted the humans to the presence of nonhumans living among them and drove them into a bloody frenzy?"

I tried to answer, but nothing came out of my throat.

Saoirse answered for me. "A collection of videos. Someone posted it on the internet. Contained tons of footage of legitimate paranormal activity. Werewolves. Witches and wizards. Vampires. Faeries." She gripped the fabric of her pants, face drawn tight in anguish. "The people in the videos were doxxed, names and addresses provided in the captions. Because the bizarre and violent nature of many of the videos spurred the FBI to investigate, it quickly became apparent that the content was...real." She let out a ragged breath. "Mass panic ensued."

Abarta nodded. "And who made that video, Lieutenant? Who caused all this suffering?"

Saoirse drew her lips into a thin line, bitterness pooling in her eyes. "Before today, I would've said we never found out, but I'm going to make an educated guess, based on your own words just now, that the answer is *you*."

Abarta smiled like he'd won a fucking chess game. "Correct."

My entire body shook with rage the likes of which I'd never experienced before. All this time, I'd thought the exposure footage had been the work of some underground human group who'd fallen down the rabbit hole and bitten off more than they could chew. And all this time, it hadn't even been the humans' *fault*. Of course, the purge was their fault. The war was their fault. The collapse was their fault. Regardless. But the inciting event, what started us all down this path of destruction that had led to a broken world pockmarked by radiation and shrouded in a long and miserable winter—that wasn't their fault.

It was *his*.

Abarta had intentionally set this world on a path to ruin so he could get back at the fae for a war that had ended when human civilization was a waddling toddler. And now that civilization was on life support, one faulty breath from a coffin. Over a conflict that didn't even involve Earth or the creatures who lived on it.

No matter how much I resented the fae and their callous rule of law and their cruel manipulations, I could *never* hate them as much as I reviled the Tuatha Dé Danann in this moment. Because human life meant something to the fae, however little. That was why they'd saved it. But human life meant *nothing* to Abarta.

That primal force within my magic rose up from the depths of my soul in response to the rage whipping around inside me. It hissed in my mind, *Kill him. Kill him. Kill him. Kill him!*

"You're the reason the harp ended up in Adelaide too, aren't you?" I finally managed to say.

"Ah yes," Abarta replied, "the harp was a nice little detail. I managed to smuggle it out of the Unseelie vaults a couple centuries back. I put it into circulation here on Earth to disguise its identity until such time as I needed it." He chuckled. "That was the reason I came to Kinsale, actually. The harp was out in Adelaide, so I decided to set up shop here to perform the counterspell while it was retrieved by my lovely assistant, Agatha Bismarck."

Like silk sheared in two, the air parted behind me, and I realized I'd been baited into a trap. I dodged to the right, but I was too close to the wall, too close to where Bismarck had been lying in wait beneath one of Abarta's flawless veils. The antique iron hatpin that had been meant for my heart pierced the top of my shoulder and emerged from my chest two inches lower.

Pain exploded through my entire body, knocking me off my feet. I hit the ground screaming, the iron burning through muscle and bone, a hundred million fire ants gnawing away at my flesh, eating me from the inside out. My vision went white. My hearing faded. I tasted blood and smelled death, the stench of my own scorched skin. I faintly heard Saoirse yell my name, but it was washed out by my own voice, so loud I nearly ripped my vocal chords in half.

Thoughts in tatters, I couldn't prevent the patch on my fourth glamour from evaporating, and the hole left behind destabilized the rest of it. It unraveled and fell away, revealing for the first time in so many years what I really looked like, what I really *was*, the truth of my heritage on display like a brand declaring me the worst kind of criminal. I wanted to press my face against the floor and hide the marks, hide my eyes, but all I could do was lie there, vainly clutching at the hatpin that had run me through. I couldn't reach around my shoulder and pull it out. I was in too much pain, and every twitch of my muscles made it flare like a belching fire.

I clamped down on the agony as much as I could and attempted to focus my eyes on the room. Everything was off kilter, double vision, but I saw Saoirse on her knees, a sword at her throat, one of her arms twisted behind her back. She was glaring in fury at the dark elf who'd emerged from the hallway and disarmed her, her gun now lying on the floor at the edge of the circle. The elf merely stared down at her in distaste, teeth bared, threatening to slit her throat if she dared to moved.

Abarta, hands in his pockets, appeared bored as he shuffled into the circle and dropped into the chair someone had placed next to the harp. As he ran a finger down the worn wood of the instrument, he said to the air behind me, "I must say, Ms. Bismarck, that was a much bolder move than I was expecting from you. I thought for sure you'd use a charm, or hell, one of those handy guns." He jutted his chin toward Saoirse's weapon. "But an iron blade? That's quite audacious."

There was an unspoken *foolish* underpinning his words, and Bismarck caught it. She appeared from within a cloud of gold smoke—the veil must've been a charm, embedded in an object on her person—a deep frown set into her face. "What do you mean? There's no better weapon than iron to use on the fae."

"Of course not." Abarta leaned back in the chair. "I mean 'bold' in terms of risking the ire of the sídhe. They're not known for being particularly lenient on those who use iron against one of their own."

Bismarck skirted around my convulsing form, dropped to one knee in front of me, and grabbed me by the chin, wrenching my face toward the light. At the sight of the marks on my face, of the unmistakable ring of frosty silver around my pupils, she blanched. Unceremoniously dropping my head back onto the stone floor, she stood and spun around with the grace of a cracking whip, growling to Abarta, "You bastard. You knew he was half *sídhe* this whole time and didn't tell me? I sent people to off him. What if he'd actually died?" She glanced over her shoulder at me, at the pin sticking out of my flesh, the one she'd put there. "What if he dies now?"

Abarta shrugged. "I didn't tell you to stab him with iron."

"You didn't tell me not to." She wrung her hands behind her back, her loose, gauzy sleeves riding up to reveal a knife strapped to each wrist. There was also a small gun on her belt, the tip of the barrel sticking out from under the hem of her shirt. "This is a *punishment*, isn't it? For letting someone catch a whiff of the harp's whereabouts."

"No," Abarta said in a chiding tone, "this is a punishment for almost ruining hundreds of years of planning. I promised you a payout the size of which your petty human dealings could never produce, in exchange for nothing but moving a musical instrument from one location to another. And you repaid my generosity by setting a nosy half-sídhe on my trail, and an Unseelie one at that. You've stuck me between a rock and a hard place. If I kill Whelan, or make him otherwise disappear, the Unseelie *will* find out, and quickly, because the higher fae keep tabs on all their half-bloods. But if I don't get rid of him, he'll go blabbing to the sídhe about my scheme to overrun the courts in Tír na nÓg."

He stamped one foot against a symbol on the circle, and the glow of the entire construction grew brighter. "Either way, your missteps, Ms. Bismarck, have accelerated my timetable beyond my comfort zone. I'll have to organize the rest of the Tuatha Dé Danann in a matter of hours, instead of days, like

I wanted, to ensure none of the fae battalions stationed in this realm can make it back to the Otherworld in time to prevent the sacking of the capital cities." He stomped his other foot, and the circle's light grew stronger still. "And *that* is why I allowed you to share some of the risk that comes along with grievously injuring a sídhe scion."

Bismarck's red lips curled into a vicious scowl. "They'll kill me if they find out I injured him with iron."

"Not if my people win, they won't." He smiled, placid and infuriating. "So you better hope it all pans out despite your mistakes."

Bismarck was visibly shaking now, not in fear but in fury. Her fingers brushed the butt of the gun hidden by her shirt, but she didn't take hold of it. She wasn't naïve enough to think she could do harm to Abarta, much less end him. Despite all her bluster, all her conceit, she was only human, and she had no magic to her name. Abarta could render her dust just as easily as he could Saoirse.

The only thing stopping him from doing so, as a real punishment for her errors, was, I assumed, that Bismarck's assets and connections in this realm held some further use for the man. Perhaps he intended to use Bismarck's network for intelligence on fae movements here on Earth, or something similar.

Either way, Bismarck knew she was beaten. She had to take Abarta's rebuke like a tablespoon of bitter medicine. But the subtle narrowing of her eyes, that razor-sharp glare, told me Abarta had made an enemy of someone who could've been a long-term ally. Bismarck would turn on him the first chance she got.

Of course, Abarta would do the same to her the moment her usefulness ran dry. Which way the double-edged sword of their relationship ultimately swung would come down to whoever first uncovered a reason to swing it.

Abarta checked a watch on his wrist. "All right. Enough dawdling." He gestured to me, bleeding atop some of the outlying symbols and shapes of the circle. "Get him out of the boundary. He can interfere with the casting if he's inside, even in his current state."

Bismarck's mood soured more at being ordered around like a lackey, but she didn't openly defy Abarta. She backtracked, grabbed me by the legs, and dragged me outside the circle, the jerky motion jostling the hatpin still slowly eating through my flesh. I cried out again, weaker this time, more like a dying whimper than a scream. Even my magic, writhing inside me, repelled by the touch of the metal, couldn't fight the fading of my consciousness. The iron was too close to my heart. It was leaching my energy away at a startling speed.

If the hatpin wasn't removed in the next ten minutes, I was going to die.

Worse yet, I had even less time to stop Abarta from casting the spell.

When it rains, it pours, little fae, said an echo of a mocking voice slinking around behind my searing pain. *Pours until you wash away.*

CHAPTER NINETEEN

"You know what the biggest irony is?" Abarta said to me as he wrote with his finger on the wood of the harp a list of softly glowing words, the names of all those he sought the harp's song to reach. "If the faerie queens, and the ancient forebears of the other nonhuman societies, hadn't instituted the universal gag rule that forbade all creatures from revealing themselves to humans, then this whole 'collapse' business would've never come to pass. Humanity would've already had a war with the nonhumans, way back when their most powerful weapons were bows and spears. And such a war the nonhumans would've resoundingly won. You all shot yourselves in the foot by holding your tongues until the humans had nuclear weapons at their disposal."

I struggled to gather enough breath to speak, and rasped, "What would your plan have been then, if there were no more secrets and lies between humans and paranormals? If the paranormals had had a greater hold on global society? What other atrocity would you have sparked? And would it have had fewer casualties, or more?"

Abarta finished scrawling his list. "To which casualties are you referring, human or other?"

"Both."

"You know, for someone who was victimized by humans, you seem strangely concerned about their well-being." His gaze flicked to Saoirse again, who shot him a glare like smoldering cinders, a promise of pain to come. He only smirked at the fleeting threat as he returned his attention to me. "You're even still friends with some of them, while most nonhumans now move in their own circles. Either you're an extremely forgiving person, Whelan, or you are quite the sentimental fool, trying to rebuild bridges best left burned to ash. Do you really think humans are worth saving, after all they've done?"

"Far more than I think the Tuatha Dé Danann are worth resurrecting from their shallow graves," I replied.

Abarta frowned. "Don't you dare compare us to *them*."

"All creatures are comparable." I had to take a wheezing pause. "Especially so with humans. Because all species with half a mind have their own special brand of pettiness, just like human beings do. It's a consequence of sentience, the potential to make stupid choices, and more so, the potential to knowingly and intentionally commit unforgivable acts. The Tuatha Dé Danann are no exception to that rule." I had half a mind to spit at him, but I didn't want to risk spitting blood, so I added, "You're a fine example of that."

Anger flickered across his gold-flecked eyes, and he rose from his seat beside the harp. As if on a string, my body jerked into the air, feet hovering an inch above the floor, and then abruptly shot toward Abarta. He caught me by the neck, fingers tightening like a noose, cutting off my airway so effectively that panic thundered up my spine and choked its way from between my lips. I clawed at his wrist with my right hand—my left wasn't responding, hanging paralyzed by the iron pin—but his hold was stronger than titanium. I couldn't even scratch his skin.

"Vince!" Saoirse attempted to stand, but the dark elf pinning her down nicked her neck with his blade. Blood welled up and trickled to her collar, soaking it red. Saoirse stared at the elf in utter disdain but didn't try to get up a second time. She wouldn't be able to help anyone if she was dead.

Abarta drew my slowly suffocating body closer to his own and held me at eye level as he spoke. "You're quite impertinent, considering the situation you're in. I'm not sure if that's the haughtiness of your higher fae blood breaking through your remaining glamours, or if it's the inherent recklessness of your human side, but I'm quickly growing tired of your antics and your wit."

His grip tightened all the more, and my vision dimmed at the edges. "I admit you played a fair game, particularly with that trick where you bounced to the Endless Sea to escape my svartálfar guard. But please understand, Whelan, that you were never a serious threat to my success in casting this spell, only to the order of events that will occur afterward. And because you chose to come here and attempt to recover the harp yourself, instead of reporting my actions to the queens, all in the name of protecting your pitiful ruin of a city, you lost any chance you had of saving the faerie capitals. They'll burn bright right along with Kinsale." He bent his smile into another sneer. "You failed, Whelan. The game's over. I won. You lost. And—"

An orange cat wearing a tie raced into the room, followed by the barghest.

The cat fit through the main door with ease, streaking across the room and bolting through a much narrower door that led into an earthen tunnel—another secret passage. But the barghest, by virtue of being the size of a truck, fit through the main door about as well as a wrecking ball. It smashed through the frame and wall as if the wood and stone were cardboard, heavy debris careening across the room.

One piece of concrete struck the dark elf in the head so hard it nearly tore his face off. He spun away from Saoirse, dropped his blade, and collapsed in a bloody wreck. Saoirse herself only missed getting nailed by a lethal projectile because she was kneeling. At the sight of the giant dog monster blasting by her, less than a foot away from crushing her beneath its massive paws, she flattened herself to the floor, covered her head, and rolled away.

The barghest lost control of itself on the turn toward the narrow door, skidding across the magic circle and tearing up numerous symbols and lines that Abarta had etched directly into the concrete. It crashed into the wall so hard the entire room shook as if struck by a powerful quake. Cracks spread across all four walls, the ceiling, and the floor. The house atop the basement groaned as the foundation shifted. The barghest, dazed by the impact, struggled to get to its feet, rocking back and forth, eyes unfocused.

Abarta, stunned, dropped me beside the harp and furiously marched toward the barghest. "You stupid hound! What the hell are you doing, chasing a cat? Your quarry is right here!"

Floating in an ocean of pain, I managed to turn myself over—the sharp corner of something in my pocket jabbed me in the side, yet another pinprick—and then I reached out toward the harp. As my fingers brushed the wooden base, I searched my beleaguered mind for a spell that could destroy it quickly, before Abarta noticed what I was doing.

A shadow loomed over me.

Bismarck, now sporting a bloody cut on her cheek, and wielding yet another enormous hatpin. Fear jolted through me at the thought of suffering another iron wound, and I desperately grabbed at anything I could find. My pants pockets, containing nothing of value. My coat pockets, containing my gem chit bag and...the object that had poked me in the side a moment ago. An object I'd forgotten all about.

"You're not that sly, Whelan," Bismarck said as she inched closer, pointing the pin toward my face, threatening to gouge out my eye. "If you think I'm going to let you ruin what little I 'did right,' then you're sore—"

A gunshot rang out.

Bismarck stumbled sideways and gasped, hand flying up to clutch her chest. She stared down in shock as bright red blood pulsed from the bullet hole near her sternum. She babbled out incoherent words, thick with pain and disbelief, before she dragged her gaze across the room to find a police lieutenant on one knee, holding a smoking gun. Saoirse, who had recovered her gun from the edge of the magic circle, didn't flinch when she made eye contact with Bismarck. Didn't show any emotion at all, except cold indifference, as she pulled the trigger a second time and shot the Duchess of Crime in the gut.

Bismarck collapsed.

Abarta spun away from the barghest, rage smoldering on his face as he took in the sight of the bleeding mob boss and traced her wounds back to a plucky cop. Growling, he raised his hand and pointed at Saoirse. Energy gathered around his fingers, a spell to wipe her from the face of the Earth. The first syllable of that lethal spell rolled off his tongue—

—at the exact same instant I ripped a folded piece of paper from my pocket and tossed it toward the harp. At the brush of paper against worn wood, I whispered the single word to strip my suppression spell from the conflagration charm that someone had stuck on the bent-up fence of my old and broken home.

The charm activated.

And the harp went up in flames.

"No!" Abarta bounded for the harp while I agonizingly rolled away from the growing plume of fire consuming the instrument. He attempted to create a vortex around the harp that would suffocate the flames. But before he finished building it, one of the harp strings snapped with the sound of a hundred mirrors shattering at once. And raked across his face.

Abarta reeled back, shrieking. Blood poured from the laceration that had split his left eye in two and sheared his skin clean through. He staggered away from the harp as the flames grew stronger still, licking at the ceiling, the support beams catching fire.

Magic older than the pyramids, imbued into the ancient instrument, began to grow and bulge and burst from random places on the harp, as the flames of the conflagration charm ate into the underlying structure. The discharges struck like lightning bolts, slamming into the ceiling, the walls, the floor, damaging the cracked foundation further. Half the room shifted five inches down as it sank into the damp earth, unsupported. The house above began to shudder and moan, louder and louder as the seconds ticked by.

Saoirse hurried to my side, eyes already tearing from the smoke. "We need to get out of here."

"Pull the pin." I shifted so she could grab the hilt.

"What? You could bleed out."

"Pull the fucking pin!"

She grabbed it, hesitated for a fraction of a second, and yanked it free.

Sweet relief flooded my system as the iron's touch released me. I rolled to my feet, more than a little wobbly, a deep ache in my shoulder that hinted at scars to come. But I was stable enough to stand, stable enough to run, if only just. I grasped Saoirse's wrist, tugged her toward me, and tossed her over my shoulder like a sack of flour. She flailed, yelping, "What the hell are you doing?" But I didn't have time to explain, didn't have time to argue.

The basement was filling with smoke. The fire was spreading. Wayward magic lightning bolts were striking everything their gnarled fingers could reach. And there were twenty goddamn svartálfar racing down the hall. So I rocketed off across the room with Saoirse in tow and lunged through the narrow door that let out into the unfinished tunnel, leaving behind a fiery harp that had become a ticking time bomb.

Thick, choking smoke rode on my heels as I raced through the darkness of the tunnel, praying there were no tripwires ahead, because I didn't have time to stop. I could sense a massive buildup of energy in the harp, a reactor reaching critical mass, seconds from overloading. I pushed my quaking legs as hard as they could go, running even faster than I had when the ghouls were in pursuit. The burst of energy from the pin removal was rapidly fading, sapped by my body's need to heal the wound in my shoulder as quickly as it could, the internal erosion of my muscles and bones severe. But I didn't stop. Didn't even think to stop. *Do not die. And do not let Saoirse die!*

Finally, a light at the end of the tunnel. The barely there glow of the full moon obscured by cloud cover. Cast down through a hole in the ground through which a ladder had been run. I skidded to a stop in front of it and practically threw Saoirse onto the ladder, screaming, "Climb!" She didn't object. She scaled the ladder while I glanced behind us, the glow of fire bright and deadly even this far from the room. The magic bomb was reaching its peak, an audible pulse in the air that even human ears could hear.

Get out of here. Now. Fast.

Saoirse rolled away from the opening at the top. Instead of climbing after her, I jumped straight up with one last great push of energy from my nearly liquid legs. I flew past the opening, and Saoirse caught my arm and yanked me away from the tunnel. I landed on my feet somehow, and then the two of us stumbled into a sprint across another dead yard surrounding another dead house, vaulted a short wooden fence, and kept on going, and going, and going, and going, and—

The house that had been Abarta's base exploded.

We were almost six blocks away, but the shockwave was so violent it threw us ten feet forward, sending us sprawling across a muddy yard. I landed face first in a puddle and came up sputtering. Saoirse, lying next to me, groaned in pain as she clutched her now dislocated shoulder. Behind us, an enormous field of fire that looked not unlike a nuclear blast gave way to a monstrous cloud of billowing slate-gray smoke.

Charred debris rained from the sky for miles around, all that remained of the house and everything inside it. I didn't have to see to know that a gaping crater had consumed the earth for at least fifty feet in every direction from the epicenter.

"Saoirse," I said hoarsely, "besides the arm, are you okay?"

Her expression was pinched, but she nodded anyway. "Maybe a cracked rib or two, but other than that, just some bruises. I'll be all right." She eyed my shoulder. "What about you?"

"Glad you asked"—my arms gave out, and I splashed back into the puddle—"because I'm done for the night."

"Vince?" She crawled over to me. "Hey, I need you to stay awake. I don't know how bad your internal damage is, and if you're not…Vince?"

I wasn't listening to her. Or anything else. Between two iron wounds, one of which was serious, and the overexertion of my injured body, my energy had finally run out. Even my magic, wild and wrathful, couldn't pump more power to my bones. My eyelids grew heavy. Saoirse's voice faded to a faint hum. Her hand shaking me, trying to rouse me, was nothing but the sensation of rocking on a gentle sea. The world around me dissolved into darkness, and my awareness fell away.

It'll be a miracle, I thought in the moment before I couldn't think at all, *if I wake up again.*

CHAPTER TWENTY

I woke up again.

It felt like I was slowly floating toward the surface of a pond until I broke through with nary a splash, eyes drifting open. The ceiling above me was unfamiliar, heavily patched and painted white. The thick, downy comforter and quilt that had been drawn up to my neck were nothing you could've scrounged from either my living area or the store beneath it. I dragged my gaze to the right to find a window, blinds drawn up to reveal a chilly day encumbered by a snow shower, flakes steadily fluttering down from the rolling gray clouds in the sky. Only the upper floors of the neighboring buildings were visible from my position, but I could tell I wasn't anywhere near home.

A door squeaked open, and I turned my head to find Christie Bridgewater shuffling into the room. She held a tray that sported a nice china teapot, a matching teacup, and a plate of saltine crackers. When she noticed I was awake, she came to an abrupt stop, shot me a sour expression, placed her free hand on her hip, and said, "Well, look who finally decided to return to the land of the living. And here I was wondering if I should make your funeral arrangements."

"Um, sorry?" I attempted to say, but my voice was a gravelly whisper.

Christie shook her head and brought the tray over, sitting it on the nightstand next to the bed. She poured a cup of steaming tea. "Once we get you situated, I want you to try a few sips of this. It's a soothing blend. Should make your throat feel better after all that screaming you did the other day."

"Screaming?" I hunted for memories of recent events, and found the equivalent of a soggy pile of newspapers sitting where they should've been. It took a great deal of effort to pry them apart and read the blurred ink. *Oh.* Abarta. Bismarck. The harp. The explosion. "Shit. Is Saoirse okay?"

"Your lieutenant friend is fine. She's overseeing the police search of Kinsale's new *crater*." Christie sat the teapot down and leaned toward me, looking for the best angle to give me leverage to sit up. I was about to tell her I could sit up without her help, when I remembered Bismarck had stabbed me with a knifelike iron hatpin.

I tugged down the collar of the loose nightshirt someone had loaned me and found my shoulder bandaged with crisp white gauze. A focused stare revealed that, underneath the gauze, someone had woven a healing spell into my skin, which explained why I didn't feel any pain. Saoirse must've taken me to a magic practitioner after I passed out.

"Crater, huh?" I said, releasing my collar. "And how did the 'mayor' and his entourage respond to that? They're not calling in the cavalry, are they? Sending in soldiers?"

"Not that I've heard." Christie tucked her arms under my torso, and with a gentle push, helped me into a sitting position. "But then, I'm not the one with the sídhe connections, so I don't have access to insider information." She cocked an eyebrow. "Like somebody I know."

My heart skipped a beat. I smacked a hand against my cheek, like I could feel the swirling silvery marks inked into my skin. I searched my chest for my glamour necklace, only to locate it sitting on the nightstand next to the tray. Four of the six charms were devoid of magic.

Shit. I forgot. My fourth glamour had failed when Bismarck stabbed me, which meant that Saoirse, along with anyone else who saw me in the aftermath, knew the truth about my heritage.

"Oh, wipe that glum look off your face," Christie said, rolling her eyes. "I'm not throwing you in the gutter just because you've got some of that fancy faerie noble blood, and neither is your lieutenant. Also, your bartender told us he already knew, so the truth is peanuts to him."

"Bartender?" I asked. "You mean O'Shea?"

"Who do you think your lieutenant called for help? Obviously, she realized you didn't want your heritage to be public knowledge—and I don't blame you for that, given the way everybody panics when one of those sídhe steps foot in town—so she looked through your phone contacts and called the two of us to come help move you to a witch's house for treatment." Christie handed me the teacup. "And before you ask, the witch promised to be discreet too. She seemed like a nice enough lady. She ordered a large batch of tea from me after she was done working on you."

"Oh, is that how you judge someone's character?" I

chuckled, uneasy. All the effort I'd put into ensuring no humans in Kinsale knew what I really was, that my mother was one of the ageless and powerful sídhe, one of the Unseelie nobles who'd crossed the veil and conquered Earth in Mab's swift and brutal campaign to end the war and its destructive nuclear bombardment…and I'd thrown it away in a scant few minutes because I let Abarta bully me into a trap.

Shame blossomed in my chest, a voice in the back of my head chiding me for such a pathetic failure. Sure, Saoirse and Christie were trustworthy—perhaps even more so than a tightlipped bartender like O'Shea—but the more people who knew my secret, the more likely it was to escape through the tiniest holes and spread through public knowledge like wildfire. And if everyone in Kinsale found out about my heritage, then no one in this town would ever do business with me again. The public was too scared of the aes sídhe. The obliteration of DC had taught them the higher fae were beings of great and awful power, godlike warriors to be feared.

And I was half of one of them. Which made me wholly a person to avoid.

I'd lose my business, and wouldn't be able to find work elsewhere in the human sphere. Which meant I'd have to slink off to the local fae government to bum a job off the very people *I* wanted to avoid…

Christie smacked me in the head with a paper towel. "For god's sake, Vince, stop acting like your puppy just died. There's no point in moping over a fear that something *might* happen. Nobody, except three of your friends and a single witch, knows you're a noble faerie boy. And it's going to stay that way for the foreseeable future. So chin up and be happy that you heroically saved the city from catastrophe." She grasped my wrist and forcibly pushed the hand holding the cup toward my mouth. "And drink your goddamn tea."

I took a sip—it was a mild, slightly sweet tea of some kind, and it did in fact make my throat feel better—my worries not quite assuaged but at least dampened for the time being. If only because Christie had no problem ramping up her tough love advice if you resisted being rational.

"So," I said, "anything happen while I was out?"

"If you mean anything important, not really, besides widespread speculation about the explosion that rattled the entire city and left a massive crater behind. Your lieutenant gave a statement to the fae bureaucrats behind closed doors—don't know what she admitted and what she left out though—but the general public is still in the dark." Christie glanced out the window, at the strengthening storm. "I'm assuming there will be a cover story making the rounds in a few days. A gas main explosion. A lone terrorist bomber. Something like that. Doubt they'll tell the truth about that Abarta guy. Seems like an issue the fae would want to handle internally."

"Did they find his body? Or Bismarck's? Or the *barghest's*? Or, well, anything left of the basement?" The blast had been so powerful, anyone inside would've likely been vaporized if they hadn't put up one hell of a shield. Or bailed into the Otherworld at the last second.

"We did not," said a voice from the doorway. Saoirse. Decked out in snow boots and a thick coat, hair and clothes dusted with snowflakes. Her right arm was in a sling, and she had a few cuts and bruises on her face and neck, but otherwise, she looked to be in good shape. Better shape than me, at any rate. "Everything in a one-block radius of the house was completely destroyed," she continued, "and what little intact debris we found contained no traces of organic matter. No blood. No tissue. So there's no way to tell who—or *what*—died in the explosion, and who, if anyone, managed to escape in time."

"Abarta got fucked up by the harp," I said, taking another sip of tea, "but I seriously doubt he let it blow up in his face. He probably jumped through a portal beforehand."

Which meant he'd be back at some point to once more try and raise the Tuatha Dé Danann from their eternal sleep, using a method far more obscure and challenging than the magic of an ancient power object like the harp. He'd also be back, I knew without a doubt, to get revenge on the impertinent half-fae who'd deprived him of a much easier victory. Me, a thirty-two-year-old former cop with a few magic tricks up my sleeve, versus Abarta, a millennia-old trickster god of the Tuatha Dé Danann.

I had made a poor choice for an archenemy.

Christ. Why do I always have to be the underdog?

"What about the mob lady?" asked Christie as she topped up my teacup even though it was still half full. "Shouldn't you be able to tell if she survived or not, based on the behavior of her underlings? Won't there be a power struggle if she's dead, to decide who takes over as the head honcho?"

"That's the thing," Saoirse said warily, scratching at a scabbed cut on her chin, "Bismarck's operations have gone dark. I've had guys checking out all the usual haunts, the restaurants and pawn shops, and all the other money-washing businesses. Most of them haven't opened since Bismarck's disappearance. I don't know whether that means she's dead and there's infighting among her captains behind the scenes, or whether they've been ordered to go underground to obscure the fact she's still alive. Regardless, the fae are now aware of her connection to Abarta. So if she resurfaces, either here in Kinsale or in another protected city…"

"They'll snuff her out, no questions asked," I finished. "The fae don't take kindly to such slights."

"Who do you think's going to fill the power vacuum," Christie asked, "if she's gone for good? One of the other big-name mobsters? Some new kid on the block?"

"Remains to be seen," Saoirse said, "but rest assured, I'll be watching. Oh, and you should also expect some announcements about increased border security and more extensive entry/exit checks. Our dear faerie mayor has decided it would be a good idea to stop people from importing dangerous objects into the city, particularly objects of Otherworld origin."

I let out a dry laugh. "Of course. I prevent another war between the fae and their most powerful ancient enemies, and I get repaid by the faerie bureaucracy with a new set of rules that'll make my day job harder. Can't wait for those bone-shaking dullahan pat-downs in search of contraband hidden in my pants."

Saoirse held up her hands in mock surrender. "If you want to make a harassment complaint, you're out of luck. The PD doesn't have jurisdiction over the horsemen."

"The PD doesn't have jurisdiction over much of anything," I pointed out.

She frowned. "We're doing the best we can."

"Didn't say you weren't. Just highlighting the sad state of affairs."

Somewhere below us, a doorbell rang.

Christie jumped. "Oh damn. My lunch break is over. I need to reopen the store. If you need anything, Vince, just shout." She scuttled out of the room and trundled down a staircase, heading into the teashop that made up the bottom floor of her building.

Now that we were alone, Saoirse sat on the mattress beside me, openly examining the marks on my face. The ones I had weren't nearly as intricate as those of the full-blooded sídhe, but they were still rather pretty. A series of delicate curving lines around my eyes and across my cheeks that both marked my blood lineage and signified my inherited power. A high scion of the Unseelie court, winter in my veins. Saoirse traced them with her gaze, her fingers twitching like she wanted to touch. She refrained because she respected my boundaries, my sensitivity on this issue I had lied to her, to everyone, about.

She finally made eye contact. If my eyes as blue as icebergs overturned, with frosty rings around the pupils, intimidated her in any way, Saoirse did not let it show. Instead, she said, "You know, before the collapse, when we worked together day in and day out, I always had this feeling, in the back of my mind, that you were hiding something. At first, before I knew about the paranormals, I thought you were just another private person suppressing personal ghosts. After I found out you were half fae, that day at the precinct where…" She bit her lip. "When I found out you were a paranormal, I thought then I really knew what you'd been hiding all that time. But still, I wasn't quite there yet, was I? I still didn't know the real Vincent Whelan."

"What makes you think you know him now?" I replied wistfully.

"I didn't *say* I know you now. In fact, I'm pretty sure this"— she brought her fingers close to my cheek but still didn't touch me, drawing the shapes of my marks in the air—"is just the beginning of a long and complicated story you're not ready to tell. My point is that I don't *expect* you to tell that story, not if you're uncomfortable with it, and that until you're ready, I won't pry. Because I know that'll drive you away."

She sighed. "I really do want to know you though, Vince, for real this time, no secrets. I want us to be friends without heavy curtains hanging between us, keeping the whole truth from getting through. And I don't want you to feel like you have to be a certain way, be a certain *kind* of person, to have a relationship with me."

She smiled the way that people did when they recounted all the things they'd lost. "I don't care if you're one of the sídhe. I don't care if you're something else entirely." Her hand drifted lower and brushed my shirt, ghosting over the bandages beneath. "You don't have to hide from me."

Of all the things Saoirse could've said, she had to say the one thing that made me cry.

Because I'd been hiding from people my entire life. Humans. Paranormals. Other fae. Because in each case, revealing the whole truth would have had consequences I couldn't bear to face. Revulsion. Fear. Panic. Betrayal. I'd spent my life standing on a glass floor, waiting for one of those great weights to drop and shatter the ground beneath my feet and send me tumbling into an abyss I couldn't escape from. And it had almost happened once, the day I'd been discovered at the precinct, the day I'd been left to die in an alley, wrapped in iron. The only reason I hadn't fallen into that hole was because Saoirse had been there to save me.

And here she was again. Offering another helping hand.

"Vince..." she said. "You okay?"

I planted my face against her good shoulder and just let

it out, faint sobs and fat tears, years of pain dripping out, one streak down my cheek at a time. I had wounds that wouldn't heal no matter who offered me kindness or how much, but the fact someone was willing to help me at all, in this scarred and broken world of scared and broken people—that was a miracle I hadn't expected. I thought I'd left Saoirse behind with the rest of my ruined past.

She embraced me, gentle as always, one hand rubbing my back. "Hey now, don't forget you owe me that date."

I didn't quite let out a genuine laugh, but it was close enough. "One fancy dinner, coming right up. As soon as I can walk again without tripping over my own two feet."

CHAPTER TWENTY-ONE

Two days later, Christie released me from her care with a warning that she would drown me with tea if I ever made her help carry my bleeding body across Kinsale again. I was tempted to point out it was Saoirse who'd called her, and that she hadn't been forced to do anything, but I had already pressed my luck enough by dropping out of this week's Scrabble match so I could recuperate. As such, I left her shop through the back door and headed home with my head hung low and a box of teabags tucked under one arm.

It had kept on snowing in spurts and fits during my time lying prone in Christie's guest bedroom, and without working snowplows, the drifts were growing high across the streets. Some valiant citizens were shoveling sections of sidewalk outside the more popular businesses, like grocery stores and convenience stores and other places you'd buy necessary supplies. But for the most part, another short stretch of deep winter had taken over the city. Though the wind didn't chill me like it did most, I still shuddered when a frigid gale blew by.

Snowstorms meant Mab was focusing her power on your region. Usually, it was because the radiation was beginning to leak beyond the containment zones she'd erected, and she needed to use some extra magic to scrub that leakage from the air and the earth and the water before it traveled too close to any protected cities. But I had an odd feeling in my chest as I crunched along through the snow today, a feeling that Mab was focusing not on the Raleigh radiation zone, but on Kinsale itself. Word of Abarta's attempted coup must have reached her ears.

Had Abarta still been here, that would've meant grave danger for Kinsale. But there had been no sign of him since the harp went up in smoke.   ·

As I closed in on my neighborhood, that shiver in my spine grew stronger. I had the sudden urge to take an alternate route and come up the narrow street behind my house, enter via the fenced-in back yard, instead of using the front entrance like I usually did. I paused, wondering why a dozen dull alarms were going off in my head, vague warnings whispered in dark corners. I was peering straight down the main street, and there wasn't a soul for three blocks down. There could've, however, been someone hiding under a veil. Like one of Abarta's perfect veils.

Now you're being paranoid, Whelan. No way he'd show his face here with the fae looking for him. He's not stupid, I tried to reassure myself. *And he can't send the barghest after you either, because if it gets caught, it'll give him away.*

But the compulsion to turn left and cut through my

neighbor's yard to reach the back street didn't dissipate. It grew stronger. So strong, in fact, that I was already moving that direction before I registered my brain giving my legs the command. I quickly trudged through the knee-deep snow and made a wide arc around a half-collapsed shed to reach my fence.

The fence was decorative, not a security measure. It was half my height, and the latch didn't have a lock. But that didn't matter because my house was warded to the teeth, so I'd left it as it was, all peeling white paint and bloated boards. Now, I glared at the ground before the fence in annoyance as I kicked the thick layer of snow away from the gate—I had to be slow and methodical about it, because the pain-reducing spell in my shoulder had lost most of its power—then brushed more snow from the latch, which was of course frozen shut. I broke the ice with a couple raps of my knuckles, finally pulled the gate open, and looked up toward my porch...

There were fifty fucking *cats* in my back yard.

And they hadn't been there a minute ago, when I first looked down to work on the gate.

I shuffled into my yard, scanning the cats from left to right. They were all colors and sizes, pure white to pure black to calico, young kittens to fully grown adults. Every last one of them was sitting the exact same way. Turned at the precise angle so it could stare at me with a fixed expression, eyes wide, pupils narrow. I looked side to side several times, waiting for one of them to do something, attack me maybe, driven by a spell. But they didn't budge. They just sat there silently, unmoving, exactly the same, except...except for the orange tabby in the middle.

He stood out from the rest because he was holding something in his mouth. A tie.

No. Not *a* tie. *My* tie. The tie I'd taken off and let float down the flood tunnel when I was fleeing the barghest.

I rewound to the night of the fight with Abarta, a hazy memory half melded to all the rest, scratched and blurred by the pain of an iron wound. Out of nowhere, an orange tabby had run through the basement, with *my* tie around its neck, being pursued by the barghest. The interruption of the barghest crashing through the door and into the wall had been the critical factor that allowed Saoirse to get her gun back and shoot Bismarck, and had allowed me to toss the conflagration charm at the harp while Abarta was distracted. If it hadn't been for that cat, the cat now sitting in my yard, still holding my tie, Abarta would've *won*.

But the cat wasn't a paranormal creature. It was a regular cat. They all were. So were they being controlled, or…?

The hairs on the back of my neck bristled.

Someone was behind me.

I broke my third glamour to release my magic, but I didn't turn around. Not yet.

Answers were beginning to slide into empty slots in the mental puzzle I'd been assembling since I first realized I'd been baited into hunting for a magical object instead of the mundane variety.

I flipped further back through my memories, to my arrival at home after handing off Walter Johnson's scrapbook. Tom had shown up less than a minute after I walked through the door, like he'd been waiting for me—or following me. And the things he'd said, his oh-so-careful conversation, framed like that of a frazzled boy yet constructed precisely so he didn't need to lie. (*An* aunt, he'd said. Not *my* aunt.) Because he couldn't lie. It wasn't in his nature.

I jumped forward to the next morning, when I started working on Tom's case. As I'd walked to Mo's, an orange tabby walked alongside me for some time, almost as if it was watching my progress. And, of course, it had been. It had been watching me the whole time. Right up until the moment I'd hopelessly lost the fight with Abarta, paralyzed by iron, and needed a helping hand to turn the tables.

From the moment I stepped back across the boundary into Kinsale the other day, I'd had eyes on my back. And not just any eyes. *How could I have been so stupid? I should've realized sooner.*

"It's impolite," I said, words buffeted by the gusting wind, "to step onto someone's property without permission, even for a free-roaming faerie like a cat sídhe."

"But I'm not stepping," said a voice smooth as torn silk, a voice that vaguely resembled the one he'd used when pretending to be a human named Tom. "I'm sitting. Is that also impolite, Vincent Whelan?"

Finally, I gathered the courage to turn around.

Perched on the fence gate was a creature that resembled Tom the human. Same height. Same weight. Same build. But the hair that had been a rich brown was now streaked with patches of black and red. And the face that had been smooth and round was now angular and severe. And the eyes that had been a soft hazel, wide and watery, were now an acid green, the pupils within them the same thin slits as the cats sitting cozy in my yard. And his smile, that horrible smile, a wound slashed across his face, revealed a set of prominent fangs where shorter canines should've been.

I *remembered* this creature, a brief flash of him, a memory hidden somewhere in the murky sea of my forgotten childhood. His unmistakable smiling face cutting through the fog, clear as crystal, even though the rest of the memory was as faint as ink left to fade under a harsh sun. I had met this creature, however briefly, maybe even spoken to him, young as I had been, unable to comprehend the weight of interacting with such an ancient, awesome force.

My lips parted, and I breathed out, "Tom Tildrum. King of the Cats."

Not just *a* cat sídhe. *The* cat sídhe.

He bent forward and threw his arm across his waist—a bow. "So fun to speak with you again, Vincent Whelan, without wearing a necessary mask."

"Don't you mean 'nice' to speak with me?" I said, unable to come up with anything better.

Tildrum blinked. He had a third eyelid. "No, I do not. I mean fun."

I licked my chapped lips. "Fun isn't also nice?"

"Not in the way that faeries use 'fun' and humans use 'nice.'"

"Oh." I swallowed, throat like sandpaper. "I see."

"No need for such a nervous look. I am not here to lecture, but rather to congratulate." He clapped. Twice. Loudly. "Queen Mab sends her regards for a job well done in preventing Abarta of the Tuatha Dé Danann from waking his kin with Daur Dá Bláo."

The gears in my brain ground to a halt. "What?"

"Do you not understand?" He dropped his hands, interlocked, into his lap. "I can provide a more in-depth explanation, if you wish."

"Yes," I choked out. "I need one."

"Very well." He ran a rough tongue across his lips. "Queen

Mab was recently made privy to intelligence that suggested a rogue member of the Tuatha Dé Danann was in the process of acquiring the harp of the Dagda for purposes that ran counter to the goals of the Unseelie Court. I was sent to recover, or destroy if necessary, the harp, as the cat sídhe were responsible for its security up until it was stolen two hundred forty-seven Earth years ago, and Queen Mab preferred that I redeem myself."

For a fraction of a second, his smile morphed into something so mindbendingly demonic that I couldn't even describe it using human words. And then the regular wicked smile was back. Just like that. And he continued, "However, I arrived too late to stop the harp from being smuggled into Kinsale, and my initial covert attempt at uncovering its exact whereabouts within the city limits were rebuffed by Agatha Bismarck's employees. At which point I was instructed by Queen Mab to change tactics and instead seek to thwart the Tuatha rogue through an appropriate proxy." His smile grew crooked. "You."

"I am not her pawn!" I snapped, the echo carried off by the icy wind. I knew I should've been more deferential to Tildrum—he was just as menacing as Abarta, not to mention far older, a being born to a primal age and later assimilated into the fae collective—but he'd trampled over the worst of my sore spots: the suggestion that I had any allegiance to the Unseelie Court, or to the cold and calculating queen who ruled it. "And she had absolutely no justification for dragging me into this mess. You're one of the sneakiest and most underhanded faeries in existence; and I don't care if you take that as a compliment or an insult. There's no reason why you had to step back after your bribe attempt at the auction failed. You could've subverted a mere human like Bismarck a hundred thousand ways. Why didn't you?"

Tildrum raise his index finger and moved it side to side. *Tsk. Tsk.* "There are factors at play of which you are unaware, Vincent Whelan. One of those factors demanded I not directly confront the Tuatha rogue. Because my initial attempt to learn the harp's location put Agatha Bismarck and Abarta himself on alert for additional interference to their plan, I determined I could pursue the issue no further without risking the confrontation I was explicitly commanded to avoid. Queen Mab confirmed my thoughts and gave me an alternative solution."

I ground my heel into the snow. "What factors?"

He shook his head. "I am not at liberty to discuss the specifics with you at this time."

"Then next time, choose someone else to be your lackey. I'm not interested in the faerie courts' circus of deception, and I won't have a hand in its manipulations, especially not when those manipulations risk what little I have left in this world." I rolled my shoulders and straightened my back to project a level a confidence I couldn't honestly claim. Then I enunciated, clear and loud and rash, "I do not work for Mab."

This time, I hoped she *did* hear me. I hoped she heard my disdain.

Tildrum cocked his head to the side, colorful eyebrows arched. "You are correct, in the human sense. You do not 'work' for Queen Mab. You receive no financial compensation for the tasks you complete at her pleasure, understood or unbeknownst to you. But you do *help* Queen Mab. And you *assist* Queen Mab. And all actions you carry out that further her goals in some way are considered to be done in her name, whether that is your intention or not. Because you are Unseelie by blood, and an unbreakable bond with your Unseelie kin is the spiritual cost of your nature."

"By blood," I said through clenched teeth, "I am half sídhe and half human. My loyalties do not lie with the Unseelie more than they lie with humanity." I huffed out a cloud of white breath, speckled with glittering flecks of ice. "So tell Mab to leave me out of her business."

Tildrum gave me what might've been an incredulous look, or a bemused one. It was hard to tell with the cat eyes. "I will forward your request."

"It's *not* a request."

Tildrum laughed, high and grating, bow raked across a violin. "It is always a request, Vincent Whelan. For Queen Mab does not defer to commands more easily than you." His laughter crept across the neighborhood, squirming into every alley, every doorway, every tiny nook and cranny, until it sounded as if it was coming from everywhere at once, an army of tittering cats mocking me from the shadows. At the same time, Tildrum's body unraveled before my eyes to the point where he was nothing but fluttering ribbons in the air, barely holding on to a human shape. Abruptly, the ribbons were snatched by the wind, but when I looked to the right to track them as they flew away, they had already disappeared.

The laughter, however, remained.

Unsettled, I turned around. To find my yard once again devoid of cats. There weren't even paw prints in the snow to indicate they'd moved. All that remained of Tom Tildrum's show of force was my tie, lying in the snow where the orange tabby had been sitting. I marched over and snatched it up, and the second I did, the last vestiges of the ghostly laughter fell to the wailing wind.

I stared at the tie in my hand for a moment, before rumpling it into a ball and stuffing it into my coat pocket. I had a great deal of information to digest, some of it irritating, some of it baffling, some of it downright terrifying. I had a faerie queen who wanted me wrapped around her finger so she could dip me into the paint of her many plots. I had a member of a defunct order of gods with my name at the top of his hit list. I had a rekindled friendship still heavily scarred that needed tender love and care I was afraid to give because I was haunted by the past. And I had a deep and aching iron wound in my shoulder that would take months to fully heal, and all the while I'd be the weaker for it.

But at least… I thought bitterly as I slogged over to my back porch and found a leather pouch filled with twenty thousand chits sitting just inside the door. *At least I don't need money.*

I grabbed the bag, stormed up the steps, wrenched the porch door open. I took down my wards, unlocked the back door, entered my empty house. I slammed the back door shut, reactivated my wards, spent forever stripping off my boots and coat. I climbed the stairs, walked to my living room, lit a battery-powered lantern. I sank into my comfy chair, picked up the book I'd been reading, opened to the page where I left off. And that was all I did for the entire afternoon, read, read, and read some more, save for taking a dinner break and a bath. And that was all I was going to do for the duration of the foreseeable future.

Because I'd had enough bullshit for one week.

THE STORY
CONTINUES

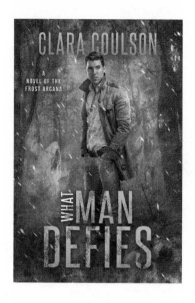

IN *WHAT MAN DEFIES*.

Out now!

LEAVE A REVIEW!

To let Clara know what you thought of *What Fate Portends*, please
leave a review!

THANK YOU FOR READING!

ABOUT THE AUTHOR

Clara Coulson was born and raised in backwoods Virginia, USA. Currently in her mid-twenties, Clara holds a degree in English and Finance from the College of William & Mary and recently retired from the hustle and bustle of Washington, DC to return to the homeland and pick up the quiet writing life.

Clara spends most of her time (when she's not writing) dreaming up new story ideas, studying Japanese, and slowly reading through the several-hundred-book backlog in her budding home library. If she's not occupied with any of those things, then you can probably find her playing with her two cats or lurking in the shadows of various social media websites.

To stay up to date on Clara's new releases, subscribe to the bimonthly newsletter: *https://claracoulson.com/newsletter/*

Made in the USA
Columbia, SC
22 March 2023

14139694R00143